HEART
OF
DEFIANCE

EVA CHASE

An Abandoned Realms Novel

Heart of Defiance

An Abandoned Realms Novel

First Digital Edition, 2024

Copyright © 2024 Eva Chase

Cover design: Mayflower Studio

Map design: Fictive Designs

Ebook ISBN: 978-1-998582-08-2

Paperback ISBN: 978-1-998582-09-9

WOUDLUND

BRYFFEN

THE SUNBLOWN SEA

THE CAPITAL
CITY OF
HEDSTOCK

SILANA

TEMPLE OF BLISSFUL
DEVOTION

ICAR

FELDAN

TEMPLE
OF THE
DANCING BREEZE

MARL TREES

VELDUNY

The Gods of the Abandoned Realms

THE ALL-GIVER (the Great God, the One) - overseer of all existence, creator of the godlen

THE GODLEN OF THE SKY

Estera - wisdom, knowledge, and education

Inganne - creativity, play, childhood, and dreams

Kosmel - luck, trickery, and rebellion

THE GODLEN OF THE EARTH

Creaden - royalty, leadership, justice, and construction

Prospira - fertility, wealth, harvest, and parenthood

Sabrelle - warfare, sports, and hunting

THE GODLEN OF THE SEA

Ardone - love, beauty, and bodily pleasures

Elox - health, medicine, and peace

Jurnus - communication, travel, and weather

CHAPTER ONE

Signy

Some people say that one person's trash is another person's treasure. I think that might be exaggerating the case a little. It's more like, one person's trash is someone else's "might as well make the best of it."

As the queen of making the best of it, I should know.

At the moment, I'm making the best of a tattered old fishing net someone discarded by the river. The rock I'm sitting on is hard against my ass, and the coarse strands of rope are rubbing my fingers raw, but the burble of the water and the light summer breeze are pleasant enough.

At least until the dukeling and his fawners show up.

I'm just knotting two of the frayed strands together, closing up a hole even the biggest trout could swim through, when their voices carry through the trees. It's easy to recognize the dukeling's. He's the one who sounds like he figures he's giving a momentous speech to the entire kingdom when his only audience is a handful of friends and the woodland creatures.

And, unwillingly, me.

The crunch of Rupert's footsteps through the brush punctuates his words. "It truly is an incredible development. I can't wait to see the reactions in our court. And naturally some benefits will trickle down to the nearest towns."

His companions' voices don't carry as much, but I catch a "That's fantastic!" and a "What a win for the duchy!" which is what they'd say even if he shat on a log.

I yank the jumble of intersecting rope into my arms, wrinkling my nose at the dank odor it gives off, but I don't manage to gather it fast enough to avoid notice. As I shove to my feet, ducking my head instinctively so my long black hair shields my face, the dukeling and three other men around my age stride up to the edge of the river where it widens about twenty paces away. Prime fishing spot—their poles gleam under the afternoon sun.

Rupert sweeps his gaze imperiously over the bank. I know he's spotted me when his lip curls with a sneer.

He flicks his blond hair away from his eyes. "Oh, look, it's the waif of refuse. I can smell her from here."

One of his lordly friends makes an obscene gesture in my direction. "Take a dunk in the river, filly, and let's see how you clean up."

The lordling next to him snorts. "It won't be well. Even her own godlen didn't want her, isn't that right?"

The last comment stings right down to the outer edges of my feet—to the stumps of the two smallest toes on each that I offered in sacrifice during my dedication ceremony when I turned twelve.

We all dedicate ourselves to one of the nine lesser gods at that age. Many of us offer up a piece of ourselves in the hopes we'll be blessed with a gift of magic in return.

Everyone else I know who offered the trade was rewarded for it.

But the gods rejected my sacrifice. Inganne, the godlen of creativity whose sigil is branded into my skin over my sternum, determined what I gave was unworthy of the magic I asked for.

So I can't even say these pricks are entirely wrong. Gritting my teeth, I ignore their jeers and grab my pouch of tools.

The fourth man in the bunch makes a disgruntled sound and motions his companions' attention back to the river. "Why bother with Signy when we've got fishing to do? That'll be a lot more entertaining than she is."

That's Landric for you. Son of the richest merchants in town, probably worried my existence will reflect badly on him in the eyes of the nobles he's sucking up to. With his striking coppery hair and well-built frame, he cuts an attractive enough figure for them to treat him as an almost-equal when they venture beyond the duke's nearby estate, but he shouldn't have any delusions that they see him as an actual friend.

Hard to believe we played together when we were little. Us and the other children around the same age clambered along this river and roamed through the woods beyond the town's last streets, explored the many crevices and caves that weave through the rocky underbelly of this landscape.

I turn my back and hurry away, biting back all the caustic remarks I'd like to make. Insulting the town outcast gets you some laughs. Insulting the duke's son and his companions gets you a dozen lashes with a whip.

I don't need to learn that lesson twice. Better to show them that I don't even care.

It's a quick tramp through the woods to the abandoned cabin I've made my own, slumped in the shadow of one of the many rocky outcroppings that jut from the forest floor. The roof is smothered with lichen and I have to stick a stone at the base of the door to hold it shut, but it's some kind of shelter.

A crack in the jutting stone marks one of the shallowest of the caves around town, a space I've turned into a storage shed of sorts. I toss the net in there to finish mending later.

A quick glance over the garden shows no new weeds have invaded since this morning. I checked my snares right before I headed to the river.

I *don't* really care about the dukeling and his views on me, but the encounter has left my nerves on edge. The little plot of land I've claimed looks even more dreary than usual.

Is this really it? This is all my life is going to be, from here until the end?

There are worse fates, I remind myself. I might as well go tend to those.

I set off on a route that skirts the edge of town, but once I reach the hill at the northern end, I have to veer onto the outer streets to make the climb. Sweat beads on my forehead with the lingering mid-day heat. I keep my gaze fixed on the polished limestone structure perched up at the top of the road, which is coming more clearly into view with every step.

A murmur catches in my ears regardless. "There goes that useless Signy."

I just keep walking.

For the last several paces of the climb, tufts of grass creep onto the packed dirt road. Really, it's more of a path at this point. I've left all the houses behind, nothing remaining but the memorial building ahead of me.

Somehow it looks less grand when standing right in front of it than it does from the bottom of the hill. I could touch the edge of the stone-tiled roof if I lifted my hands. The whole structure is barely larger than my decrepit cabin.

But no one needs to live in this building. It's a symbolic home to honor those no longer living at all.

Row upon row of names are carved into the outer walls, the earliest etchings from centuries ago worn down with age. I pick up one of the rags I keep in a bucket near the corner and start wiping away the grit and bits of moss that've attached themselves to the surface, obscuring some of the letters. Here and there, I need to take out my pocket knife to scour off the worst bits.

The names continue all the way around the back of the building and onto the other side, where the newest additions reach about halfway across. Still plenty of room for more, and no doubt there will be more to come.

I give the last couple of rows an especially thorough wipe, my gaze lingering on two names that were added sixteen and thirteen years ago respectively, when I was five and then eight.

Greta Emadaut. Faro Hendiksson.

I rest my fingertips against the carved letters, my tan skin dark compared to the pale stone.

My memories of my parents have fragmented with time, gone hazy and disjointed. But Mom's smile still beams through my recollections, alongside Dad's buoyant laugh. The way she'd cuddle me on her lap when I scraped my knee, weaving flowers and ribbons into my hair. The way he'd toss me up in the air like I weighed nothing at all and then swing us in a giddy circle.

No markings on the building say what the memorial is for. We're too afraid to openly state it.

Our conquerors don't like any hint of discontentment with their rule. If we gave away that we're bearing witness specifically to our family members, friends, and neighbors who the Darium empire's soldiers have struck down, this structure would be rubble by sundown.

It's hard to imagine what this town—what all of our country—might have been like before Dariu invaded the entire continent. The last people who experienced the old Velduny are long dead. But I have to think life was better when our kings and dukes and countesses weren't worrying more about keeping favor with their overseers than serving their own people.

I put away the rag and grab the broom to sweep off the tiles around the memorial. My gaze wanders over the landscape around the hill, and some of my earlier restlessness subsides.

It's a stunning view. The domed marble roof of our temple of the All-Giver glints under the sun, ornate patterns carved across it. Next to it, the ancient town hall looms with a subtle grandeur. Its burnished pinkish-gray stones were cut from the local hillsides.

On either side of town, winding crags rise up amid the forest like islands in a sea of green leaves. One curves right over to meet the ground again, forming the arch visitors ride through to enter town along that road.

Straight ahead to the south, our river winds through grassy plains before feeding into a sparkling lake at the foot of jagged mountains. A temple of Inganne, my chosen godlen for all she dismissed me, stands a couple of miles to the west of the lake, shining so vibrantly orange it immediately draws the eye.

Looking at it, I tap my fingers down my front in the gesture of the divinities: forehead for the three godlen of air, heart for the three of the sea, gut for the three of the earth, then fisting my hand between my breasts where I have Inganne's sigil burned into my skin. I can't not pay my respects to our gods when faced with this vista, even if they don't care much for me.

I'm still not totally sure why Inganne rejected my sacrifice. The shame of it has never stopped burning. But I am blessed to live in a place surrounded by such beauty.

I don't need to have magic to one day honor that beauty with something I've created, like I've always dreamed.

Something like the fountain burbling in our town's central square. When my attention drops to it, a couple of kids are swaying along the outer edge of the basin. The girl slips and jumps into the water with a burst of giggles. On the other side, one of the town cats darts over to lap up a little water.

My mother left her mark on this town, even though she was stolen from my life far too soon. She carved every curve of the elegant figure standing on the fountain's platform, pouring the water from a jug. Every petal on the flowers that dapple the ground around the woman's feet. Every symbol on the Veldunian crest that binds her rippling cloak.

Adelheid is an old Veldunian folk hero. It's said she gave up her home and traveled the country in a time of drought, helping those she met find ways to keep their crops and gardens alive, and Prospira, the godlen of fertility and abundance, blessed her with a jug that would never totally empty.

The corner of my lips curves up in a wry smile. I once imagined contributing a work of artistry that was even more breathtaking. Now that idea seems ridiculous. But I'm glad that Mom's creation keeps nurturing the town even after her death.

I've put the broom away and am taking one last look over the landscape when I spot a cluster of dark figures on horseback riding along the road to our natural stone archway.

There's no doubting what they are the second my eyes catch on their uniforms. Only Darium soldiers wear those outfits that are black from helm to boots—other than the white skull and bones painted onto the material.

They make themselves up to look like living skeletons. I

can't deny it's effective. A shiver travels down my back as I watch the five of them.

I stick to my high perch, following their progress into town. For a minute or two here and there, I lose sight of them amid the buildings. But it's always easy to pick them out again as soon as they pass into view.

When they reach the edge of the main square, they dismount. The nearby townspeople stiffen and slip into the nearest buildings as surreptitiously as they can manage.

One of the soldiers motions to his companions as if he's in charge, and a couple of the others march over to the bakery.

My stomach knots. I don't need to be in hearing range to figure out what's going on.

No money will be exchanging hands. The soldiers of our long-time conquerors simply point and take.

The men come out of the bakery with a couple of bundles of rolls and pastries. They lift the visors of their helms to eat, and the leader's mouth glints metallic in the fading sunlight.

He sacrificed a few teeth at his dedication ceremony for a gift. Assuming *his* sacrifice was accepted by his chosen godlen.

Which most are. I'm the rare exception.

One of the soldiers saunters over to the fountain and fills his canteen from the water streaming from the jug. Another follows him and peers up at the figure. He turns to say something to the leader.

I can't read the leader's expression from here, but he strides over to a couple of townspeople who've just jarred to a halt across the square. Before they can hurry away from the intruders, the soldier asks them something with jabs of his hand toward the statue.

What's going on? What could they possibly be upset about?

The tension in my gut winds even tighter with the sense of some impending horror. My hands ball at my sides.

Whatever the townspeople answer, the leader shakes his head. He peers up at the statue for a moment and turns to walk back to his underlings.

For the space of a few heartbeats, I think it's over. Everything's okay.

Then he waves his hand toward Mom's fountain in a flippant gesture as if to say, "Do what you like with it."

Three of the solders retrieve spiked clubs that were dangling from their saddles and barge forward. With a brutal swing, the first smacks his club down on the statue's arm.

A cry breaks from my throat. Even as the sound bursts into the air, another soldier attacks the statue, battering it with thumps that carry all the way to my hilltop. The third hangs back with a hint of hesitation, but she doesn't move to stop her colleagues either.

With a few more strikes, the statue's arm cracks. Chunks fall off the mouth of the jug, tumbling into the basin's water. The first soldier hops right onto the platform, his boots scuffing against the delicately carved flowers, and bashes at Adelheid's marble head.

The tension bottled inside me explodes through my body. It knocks every thought from my head but a silently wailed *No!*

My legs propel me forward. I'm running down the hill at full tilt, my patched boots smacking the cobblestones, my breath searing my throat.

No, no, no.

My sprint to the square passes in a blink in the haze of my panic. I'm barely aware of the buildings I'm rushing by, the road falling away beneath my feet, the instinctive splaying of my remaining toes ensuring my balance.

I careen into the square just in time to hear one of the soldiers muttering to the others. "All these years and everything we've done for them, and they still think they should celebrate the time before the empire."

He swings his club at what's now a stump of the statue's arm, and I hurl myself at him.

Somehow, my pocket knife is in my hand. I barrel into the soldier, slashing out with it, my voice crackling up my throat. "That's *ours*. You can't take it. You can't take everything!"

My knife skids over the leather covering his upper arm before tearing through the fabric and flesh below his elbow. The soldier grunts and heaves me to the side with a smack of my jaw.

I stumble and manage to stay upright, brandishing the blade, breathing hard. "Get the fuck away from our fountain. It belongs to this town, not to you."

The fact that anyone's objected at all has apparently bewildered the soldiers. All five of them have turned to stare at me, the two at the fountain momentarily lowering their clubs. The one I cut has his hand pressed to the wound, the cloth around his fingers turning even darker with blood.

"Who the fuck do you think you are?" the leader snarls, drawing his sword.

I'm too angry to be scared. "I live here. This is my home. And I don't want you here."

I launch myself at him so quickly he's obviously not prepared. Rather than push forward to meet me, he flinches backward.

My knife swings wide, but I heave my fist forward too, clocking him in the nose. He recovers with a snarled curse. I barely dodge under the swipe of his blade.

He wheels toward me, murder in his gaze, and the realization penetrates the blare of adrenaline in my veins that I might actually die today. My name might be the next added to the memorial on the hill. The other soldiers storm toward me—

And a metal bowl flies through the air to clang against one of their helmets.

"She's right!" the baker's assistant yells, wielding a steel tray like a weapon. "Get out of here and leave what's ours alone."

All at once, more dishes and other odds and ends—rocks, shoes, a hammer—pelt the soldiers along with a barrage of shouts.

"Go away!"

"There's nothing for you here!"

"Get back on those horses and ride!"

A crowd of townspeople has emerged from the buildings around the square, their faces taut with the same fury and anguish I was feeling. No one else would have wanted to see the fountain destroyed any more than I did.

They were just too afraid to say anything until someone else did it first.

"Back off," one of the soldiers growls, and jabs his club at the people closing in around him. It smacks into a little girl's jaw.

At her yelp of pain, the crowd surges forward. They punch and shove at the soldiers, heedless of their weapons.

Bertha from the butcher shop lunges forward and stabs a skewer straight into one skeleton-painted chest.

The soldier jerks and collapses, blood gushing from the wound. As Bertha yanks the skewer free, the Darium leader must decide his squadron is too outnumbered.

He doesn't have any intention of dying today.

"Pull back," he calls to his underlings, already retreating.

They hustle to the horses they left at the edge of the square and haul themselves into the saddles.

"That's right!" a woman next to me hollers. "Run like the beasts you are!"

The leader yanks his horse around. "You're going to pay for today, peasants."

Then they canter off the way they came.

A cheer goes up through the crowd of townspeople. Exhilaration rushes through my chest alongside it.

Excited voices babble all around me, friends gripping each other's arms and exclaiming over our victory. With a grin on my face, I start to ease back to the fringes.

But Bertha grabs my arm and peers at me. "Are you all right, Signy? That was impressive, the way you came at them."

As I blink at her, a man speaks up from behind me. "It really was. You showed them they can't get away with whatever they want."

An older woman who's eased into the crowd aims a quiet smile at me. "Your mother would be proud."

My voice comes out in a stammer. "I—thank you. I just couldn't stand seeing them break her fountain."

"There's a line," someone mutters.

Someone else gives me a hasty pat on the back. "You did good."

Despite the ache where the soldier bruised my jaw, a smile stretches across my face. All at once, I feel like I did as a kid, spun around giddily by Dad like maybe if I wished it hard enough, I could actually fly.

"We kicked them out," I say, barely able to believe the words. "We kicked them right out of town."

Bertha grins fiercely. "And if they come back, we'll do it all over again. Now let's celebrate our first taste of freedom in three hundred years."

CHAPTER TWO

Landric

"Here, have another!" Arette the barkeep grabs the cup I've drained and pushes a second mug of ale into my hands.

She heads off across the square, exchanging empties for newly filled vessels, with a spring in her step to match the music. A melody of lute and horns lilts through the air. Over near the players, a bunch of my fellow townspeople are bounding around in a dance of celebration under the glowing lanterns.

Gunther the baker has been distributing fresh pastries as fast as he and his assistant can bake them. Novak the farmer is handing out the pears and plums he brought to sell.

Everyone who isn't dancing is wandering around exclaiming over what a spectacular night it is. I haven't seen this many smiles on my neighbors' faces in… in possibly my entire life.

Next to me, Rupert wrinkles his nose at his own barely

touched mug of ale. He speaks with the dryly derisive edge I've gotten used to. "So this is what small town festivities look like. So... quaint. I suppose it's not your fault when you don't have much to work with."

His two noble friends guffaw. I bite my tongue.

I do so much of that around the duke's son that it's a wonder I haven't bitten right through. Rupert has a lot of opinions about my home and the people I've grown up with. Sometimes I'm not sure whether he takes the breaks from court life more to enjoy a little freedom or simply to gawk at his supposed lessers.

But I've been able to earn my way into his good graces. He doesn't see me as quite the same clueless hick as everyone else in town.

So I will just keep biting my tongue until I can leverage this association into a career that sees my mother's business secure—and me finally on my way out of this place.

Deiter, Rupert's duller regular companion, gives the crowded square a puzzled frown. "What exactly are they celebrating again? Someone fought the Darium army?"

"Not the whole army," I say. "A few soldiers were bashing up our fountain, and everyone got upset and managed to drive them off. We wouldn't usually try to stand up to them." Let alone hope to succeed.

The thought sends a quiver of excitement through me. I wish I'd been here to see the confrontation.

Even if just a glimpse of those skeletal uniforms can turn my gut into a lump as hard and cold as granite.

We only got the story secondhand after we headed into town for dinner once our fishing was done. The shadows shifting across the fountain in the lantern light show the statue of Adelheid is missing most of one arm, her nose and chin cracked off, a chunk missing from the jug that pours the water.

Looking at it sends a renewed pulse of anger through my veins. Can't they let us keep *anything*?

Rupert makes a disgruntled sound and smooths back his pale hair from his ruddy face. "It's bad business, really. Father always says we should work *with* the empire, not against them, and I agree. We'll put ourselves in a much better position in the long run."

It's not as if *he's* in a position to make any political decisions at the moment. As far as I can tell, the most responsibility Duke Berengar trusts his son with is not to drown in the river when he takes off on one of his country larks.

Deiter and Leonhard murmur in eager agreement, though, so I force a smile. "It obviously wasn't a move made out of wisdom."

Only the pure, totally justifiable craving for retribution.

I scan the crowd as if I might pick out my mother's face, even though I already looked for Mom earlier. She'll be off in the shop's back room, sorting through inventory and fretting over whether the acquisitions and sales will balance out. She might not even know anything unusual has happened.

She used to smile a lot more. Laugh, even. When she and Dad handled the business together, his sharp mind for negotiating the perfect pairing with her persuasive warmth, life felt easy.

Now I constantly get the impression that she's treading water, a few weak kicks away from going under.

I glance up toward the memorial on the hill. Even with the celebration, someone remembered to light the lantern that sends a glow over the glossy stone.

It's been seven years since we carved Dad's name into its side. Seven years since a Darium noble marched into a negotiation with a tradesman and cut Dad down for daring to bargain for what the noble had decided was already his.

We still don't really know how to live without him.

Rupert lets out a low, dark chuckle that immediately puts me on the alert. "Oh, look, there's the waif of refuse who somehow started it all."

I yank my gaze back to the crowd. Signy is just weaving past us, carrying a bucket I can't make out the contents of.

Her tan face looks strangely solemn amid the revelers, but her dark eyes burn so fiercely I can't look away. The waves of her black hair tumbling across her shoulders as wild as always only make her more breathtaking.

The lantern light glances across her face, and I spot the purpling splotch of a bruise on her jaw. My hand closes into a fist as if I could punch it into the past to smack down the prick who battered her.

Of course it would have been her who spoke up first, who launched herself at those soldiers rather than freezing up in fear. She's never let all the caustic whispers stop her from doing what matters to her.

No one's sneering at her now. Even as I watch, a couple of our neighbors raise their mugs to her in cheers, and another gives her arm a quick squeeze with a look of gratitude.

There's something delightful about the startled awe she can't quite hide beneath her wariness.

I saw her aunt and uncle among the dancers. What do they make of their niece's sudden shift in status?

No one spoke against them when they kicked her out of their home at sixteen and left her to fend for herself. Trouble enough having to take in an orphan after they'd just finished raising their own children, but one who was rejected by her godlen? Who skulked around the town like she had nefarious deeds in mind?

Who could blame them for wanting no part in that? That's what everyone murmured behind Signy's back.

Funny how one brief act could shift opinion so quickly. I only hope it doesn't swing back toward disdain by tomorrow.

She deserves better. She's deserved so much better from *me* than simply trying to divert a little hostile attention away from her.

Gods, she must hate me. She must hate all of us.

And why shouldn't she? Here I am, still playing along trying to win my own game.

"What is the bint doing?" Leonhard says, peering at Signy as she moves through the crowd toward the fountain.

Between the milling bodies, I catch a glimpse of her setting the bucket down on the rim of the basin. Several chunks of broken marble have been laid out along it nearby. She picks up the largest piece of arm and hops onto the rim to hold it to the statue's stump.

Rupert figures it out at the same moment I do. He snorts. "Of course. She thinks she can fix it. Always poking around in the trash. I suppose like calls to like."

Deiter shakes his head. "Why's that fountain matter so much anyway?"

The words jolt out of me in a sharper tone than I intended. "Her mother made it. It's the last sculpture she carved before a Darium soldier killed her."

Rupert turns his attention on me, keenly enough that my skin prickles uneasily. He keeps his voice smooth, but I can hear the undercurrent of warning. "If the woman was anything like her daughter, I'm not sure the soldier should be blamed for it. No doubt she was asking for it."

He's goading me, wanting to see if I'll react. And Great God help me, the urge to slam my fist into his smug face rushes up so fast I'm not sure I can contain it.

My shoulders stiffen with tension—and a clatter of hoofbeats breaks through the music, cutting off my anger with a startled hitch of my pulse.

Most of the crowd whirls toward the arrivals: several armed men on horseback who've drawn to a stop at the edge of the square. My heart thuds even louder in the split second before I recognize that they're not wearing the eerie Darium uniforms but the burgundy jackets and steel caps of the Veldunian armed forces. The hobbled remains of our army that our Darium overseers allow to handle local disputes.

One of the soldiers prods his horse forward, his bright blue eyes blazing in stark contrast with his bronze-brown skin. "Stop the music! Grab what you can. You need to evacuate the town *now.*"

CHAPTER THREE

Signy

An unfamiliar voice rings across the courtyard, and the musicians abruptly lower their instruments. I spin around on my fountain-side perch with a wobble of my pulse.

Did he say we need to *evacuate*?

The man leading the pack of Veldunian soldiers points across the square. "Everyone, head to the west of the town as quickly as possible. Keep going until you're well beyond the buildings. Hurry!"

With a shaky breath, I set down the bucket of supplies I brought with me. What is going on?

My uncle steps forward with his usual bluster. "Why should we leave? Are you even going to tell us what's going on?"

The head soldier lets out a strained sound, his chiseled face taut with frustration. He motions to his companions. Most of them split off to ride off through the city streets away from the square.

"The Darium army has put out an order that this town is to be burned to the ground," he says. "We're under orders to *help* them, but we'll help you as much as we can before they get here. Please, grab only what you absolutely need and leave. I don't know how far behind us they are."

My chest constricts so tightly that for a moment, I can't breathe at all. An ache spreads all the way to my ribs.

It's because of me. Because I attacked the soldiers and stirred up the rest of the town to follow my lead.

The Darium soldiers said we'd pay for it. I just had no idea—I never thought—

All sense of revelry has vanished from the square. My neighbors grab their children and run toward their houses or off to the west without stopping to collect any belongings.

We all know that when the Darium army says they're going to burn a place, they're not going to hesitate to burn up anyone still in it too.

The banging of doors and the soldiers' hollered voices carry from the nearby streets. "We're evacuating the town! You need to leave now. Everyone, quickly!"

I remain on the rim of the fountain's basin, frozen amid the panicked bustle of the crowd fleeing the square. The bottom of my stomach has dropped out.

Burn the town. My parents' old house, since claimed by another family. The homes where so many were born, grew up, made lives for themselves.

The gorgeous temple I admired just this afternoon. The grand old town hall.

My gaze darts to the memorial on the hill, and my lungs clench even tighter.

The Darium soldiers will destroy that too, won't they? They'll scorch or smash the stones with the names of the fallen, score my parents' names out of existence as if they never lived at all.

I told them they couldn't take everything that belonged to us, and they mean to prove me wrong.

Where will we go after we flee? What town will take in another town's worth of people?

The soldiers will probably hunt us down across the countryside once they've destroyed our home.

If we let them.

A sharp sear of conviction shoots up from my gut. "No!" I shout over the frantic clamor. "We stood up to them before. We showed them they couldn't bully us. We can stop them!"

As several people turn to stare, I leap off the basin and cast around.

Bertha brought out a few geese from the butcher shop to roast—carcasses are still dangling from rods near the braziers. I run over and yank out one of the pointed roasting spits.

Brandishing it in the air like a spear, I call out again. "There are hundreds of us. They won't be sending that many soldiers. If we push back, we can save our town. We don't have to let them get away with this."

Some of the townspeople keep rushing by, but others hesitate. Gunther glances back toward his bakery and then toward the fountain where our first confrontation was successful. His hands ball into fists.

Bertha marches over to me and grabs another of the spits. Fear shines in her eyes, but her jaw is set.

She raises her makeshift weapon in the air like I did. "We should fight for what's ours! Come on, everyone. I have more rods and knives in my shop. We'll batter them with frying pans and garden hoes if that's what it takes."

I might have gained a little respect from my defense of the fountain, but Bertha has been considered an upstanding citizen for a lot longer than I have. Her voice rallies far more people than mine did.

As she ushers people into her shop to arm themselves, the

head Veldunian soldier and his remaining companion ride over to us. His startlingly bright blue eyes flash with anger—and maybe a little fear of his own. "What in the realms do you think you're doing?"

I hold up the roasting spit and set my other hand on my hip, ignoring the racing of my heart. "This is our town. We can't just stand by and watch them destroy it."

He wheels his horse around. "You don't have any choice. You can't hope to push back an entire squadron of Darium soldiers."

"We sent them running this afternoon. We weren't even prepared then."

Bertha comes bustling back out of the butcher shop. More figures are gathering around us, gripping whatever makeshift weapon they could get their hands on.

Sef the farrier swings his arm. "If they're coming from the east, we have to meet them there. Gather your friends—anyone who'll stand and—"

With a distant hiss, a streak of yellow-orange light flares against the night sky at the east end of town. Flames are shooting up from the buildings on the fringes.

A chill washes through my body. Our enemies are already here.

An uneasy murmuring passes between the townspeople who gathered around me and Bertha. I can sense their resolve dwindling.

Clammy sweat trickles down my back, but I jab my spit toward the flames. "We have to face them now! They won't be expecting it. We'll strike them all down."

For a moment, I think my battle cry will be enough. My neighbors shift toward the east end of the square, grim determination crossing their faces.

The lead soldier wheels his horse, his mouth tight. "You

don't want to do this. Please, get out of the town while you can."

His companion leans over in his saddle. "Jostein, if the soldiers see us—"

"I know," the other man snaps.

Bertha and I wave our band of resistors forward anyway. We hustle across the square.

And then the first victims of the razing come pelting through the streets.

A woman clutching a baby stumbles at the edge of the square. Her hair is singed, a burn mark on her cheek.

"They're coming!" she wails. "They killed Nivard."

Her husband.

More fleeing figures dash toward us from behind her. One man has blood spreading down the shoulder of his shirt from a deep gouge. Another hobbles next to her partner, her ankle awkwardly bent. A kid who can't be more than ten sprints past them, burns bubbling on his forearms and jaw.

When he sees the bunch of us, his voice splits the air in a shriek. "The empire is here! They're going to kill all of us! Mom... Dad..."

More fire wavers all along the east end of town. The warble of it seems to come from all around us. Smoke laces the air.

A man staggers into the square and then crumples, the back of his tunic drenched in blood. His eyes stare at us blankly.

The lead Veldunian soldier rides around us, his voice even more urgent than before. "That'll be the fate all of you meet if you don't get out of here *now*."

The small spirit of rebellion we summoned disintegrates.

"Run!" Gunther cries. His voice is echoed by others in the crowd.

Even Bertha turns on her heel, grasping the burnt boy's

arm to steady him and bolting in the opposite direction from the flames. The lead soldier and his companion wave everyone onward to the streets heading out of town.

My throat prickles with the thickening smoke and the anguish that threatens to choke me. "No! We can't give up. We can't let them ruin it all."

But everyone who stood with me has rushed off. I'm alone amid a torrent of the wounded and panicked escaping the carnage.

I grit my teeth and hold my roasting spit steady, bracing my feet against the cobblestones. My pulse hammers through my limbs and in the back of my skull.

If I lose this place, the only home I've ever had, the only place that holds the memories of the family I already lost... I have nothing. What's the point in going on?

If the Darium soldiers want to fight me, let them. I'll take as many of them down with me as I can.

More townspeople careen past me. Harsher shouts of warning and retribution reach my ears.

The Darium force is getting closer.

I clutch my spit with all my strength—and a huff of breath sounds right behind me.

The lead soldier tips over on his horse and smacks his arm right around my chest. Before I can do more than gasp, he's heaved me up onto his lap, knocking aside the spit.

I sprawl on my stomach across his muscular legs, my own legs dangling. As I try to squirm away from him, he pins my lean frame against him with one arm while the other tugs on the reins.

"What are you doing?" I sputter. "I was going to—"

His thighs shift with the press of his heels, and the horse springs forward, away from the burning. The soldier's voice comes out in a growl. "I'm saving your life, as little as you seem to care about it. There's nothing else here you can salvage."

CHAPTER FOUR

Jostein

Iko glances around our hasty refugee camp. In the first haze of early dawn light that seeps between the trees, the people of Feldan huddle together, some dozing, some staring ahead in a daze. Their faces are marked with grit and soot—and here and there smears of blood.

My friend rakes his fingers back through his dark blond hair, pushing the chin-length strands behind his ears. His lips slant into a wry grin, but his voice comes out rough. "Well, this is a mess and a half, isn't it?"

I swallow thickly. "We did the best we could."

I don't know how many of the townspeople died in the Darium attack. We managed to usher a few hundred deep into the forest beyond the western edge of the town, farther than the Darium soldiers bothered to venture. From the size of the settlement and the number of buildings now smoldering in embers, I doubt this is even half of them.

But then, we're lucky we made it to the town far enough ahead of the Darium forces to warn them at all. If we'd been with the empire's squadron, they'd have expected to see us burning and murdering alongside them.

Our first loyalty is to Dariu, as our overseers so often remind us.

Iko and I meander onward in our informal patrol, Iko fiddling with a branched stick and a scrap of leather he's assembling into what looks like a slingshot. As if the sword at his hip isn't enough of a weapon.

He never knows how to sit still. Always has to keep his hands moving. I'll admit that he's come up with some ingenious solutions by seeing what odds and ends he can meld together, but this morning his fidgeting is wearing on my nerves.

A woman we pass is clutching her arm, weeping in soft sobs. I kneel down in front of her. "Are you injured? We have a medic who should be able to help."

She shakes her head. "It's just a scratch. But I got it when —I couldn't grab Maud fast enough..."

Another sob overwhelms her voice.

I straighten up with a sensation like a jagged blade in my gut. I don't know who Maud is—wife, daughter, friend—but it's obvious she meant a lot to this woman.

The cleric and a few of his devouts who escaped the burning of their temple have been offering what comforts they can to their neighbors. I'll have to direct one of them over here when we next cross paths.

As we walk on, Iko hums to himself. "We should show them a painting of Agnethe. They can feel good that they were spared that catastrophe."

His jaunty tone brings my gaze jerking to him. He catches my expression and swipes a hand across his mouth, looking abashed. "Too much? Too much. Ah, there's our spitfire prisoner. It was something watching you play hero to save her from her own heroics."

If his voice has gone droll again, I'm too distracted by the sight of the figure up ahead of us to care. All my exasperation is aimed at her.

I've gathered from murmurs and mutterings that the bloodthirsty woman's name is Signy. She didn't tell me herself, of course, because she hasn't said a word to me that's not cursing or complaint since I hauled her out of the town square.

She sits now with her arms looped around her raised knees and her head drooped, her rumpled black hair spilling down her back, but I recognize the tension still coiled in her sinewy frame. Given an opening, she'd be dashing back to Feldan in a split-second, never mind that the soldiers she'd like to flay are long gone now.

That's why there's a rope wound around her wrists and ankles, tying her to the birch tree she's crouched in front of. She already tried to run off twice before we finally put her under official arrest for resisting military authority.

That was a few hours ago. Maybe she's cooled off a little since then—enough to be reasoned with.

With trepidation winding through my chest, I walk the last several paces to stand in front of her. When she doesn't acknowledge me, I clear my throat. "Well? Have you sorted yourself out yet?"

She lifts her head, and I immediately regret drawing her attention. Those striking emerald-green eyes blaze hotter than the summer sun, searing into me as if she's peering straight through to my soul.

Her lips pull back in what's almost a snarl. "The one who needs sorting out around here is you. You call yourself a Veldunian soldier, but you're not even willing to fight for your country? You might as well take off that uniform and put on the Darium bones."

The comment sets me even more on edge in an instant.

"We're not the ones who torched your home. We did our best to warn you and get you all to safety."

Her voice rises. "We would have stood up to those assholes with sticks and pans. You're the ones with the swords, and all you were willing to do is run away."

Several gazes turn our way at her words. Even tied to a tree, she can command attention in a way that gives me a pang of mixed admiration and envy.

And the quiver in my abdomen in memory of my dedication sacrifice tells me she means it. She really would have battled the Darium soldiers to the bitter end, even alone, and probably felled a few of them in the process.

The gift Creaden blessed me with lets me judge who's up to a task, and it's usually accurate.

It and my steadfast dedication to my career haven't gotten me promoted past squad leader, though. *You're just not very... commanding*, my last captain said.

I don't think I need to be taking tips from this half-feral woman, though.

"Look," I say firmly, the back of my neck prickling with awareness of our growing audience, "the Darium empire has kept the entire continent under its thumb for centuries. Even if we fought off that squadron, they'd send more people next time. Rebellion is a death sentence. At least when we work around them instead of coming at them head on, we can protect some of you instead of encouraging what'll essentially be suicide."

"Which is not just depressing but very messy to clean up," Iko puts in, and I restrain the urge to glower at him.

Signy's gaze flicks to him and back to me. A little of the fierceness fades from her expression, and I see the exhaustion behind it.

Her next words come out quieter, but they seem to ring all through the forest in the silence our argument has cast.

"What's the point? What does it matter if you saved our lives when everything that mattered in those lives has been destroyed? Do our *breaths* even belong to us, if the only reason we get to keep living is because the Darium empire didn't decide to slaughter me or him or her today?"

She waves her hand toward the huddled townspeople as well as she can with her wrists bound.

A lump clogs my throat. I push my voice past it. "Of course it matters. You can rebuild—you can recover—you still have one another—"

Signy's eyes narrow. "Tell that to everyone here who lost someone they cared about to enemy swords last night. At least if we'd stayed and fought, the pain would go both ways. We'd have shown them that we do matter."

Last night's frustration swells inside me, overwhelming everything else I'm feeling. "You already fought. From what I heard, you all attacked a small patrol and killed one of the soldiers. Burning the town was your punishment. Was all that loss really worth it for a few minutes of 'showing them'?"

To my surprise, the woman flinches. Her head droops for a moment as she works her jaw. "It was my fault. I started the fight on my own. No, that's not really true. *They* started it by deciding to smash our fountain just because it wasn't some kind of homage to their empire. But I drew the first blood."

For a second, I can only gape at her. "You launched an attack on the patrol... by yourself?" A single, untrained woman against several fully-equipped Darium soldiers?

She grimaces. "I couldn't stand to let them ruin one more thing... I didn't expect it to go that far. I wasn't thinking. I was just so angry."

My shock steals the rest of my voice. Gods above, I'm not sure I've ever met a human being so reckless... or so passionate. It took an incredible amount of courage for her to instigate that act of resistance alone.

Of course, after seeing how she hollered for her neighbors to push back the Darium force last night, maybe I shouldn't be surprised by that.

Iko lets out a low whistle, his eyebrows lifted with similar awe. "If you get that much done when you're mad, remind me never to piss you off."

I consider stomping on his foot to shut him up, but then Signy's eyes flash toward us again. "We could have gotten a lot more done if you'd been completely on our side. All it took was me jabbing a pocketknife at the soldiers for so many other people to stand up to them too. Maybe we could have saved the whole town if your squad had rallied us instead of running us off. How do you know what's possible when no one's tried to rebel in ages?"

Footsteps crunch through the underbrush with an ominous thudding. Captain Amalia, who sent my squad and one other off on the evacuation mission, marches into view.

She frowns down at Signy. "We've heard enough out of you. Keep your foolhardy thoughts to yourself, or we'll add a gag along with the ropes."

I wince inwardly at her caustic tone, even though I was essentially trying to get Signy to do the same thing. A flurry of whispers, some supportive and some agitated, ripple through the mass of refugees around us.

Signy glares back at Amalia, but she appears to take the captain's authority seriously. Her mouth clamps shut, wary of the threat.

Then a man who can't be more than a year or two older than she is shoves to his feet from where he was sitting among his neighbors. The dawn light flares in his reddish-brown hair like the fires in town last night.

"She shouldn't have to shut up," he says, his voice pealing through the forest. "Signy's right."

CHAPTER FIVE

Signy

I'm so busy staring at my unexpected defender that the first surge of conversation rushes past me without my comprehending.

Landric stands tall and defiant, his dark brown eyes penetrating beneath the sweep of his coppery hair. He's staring down the soldiers rather than looking at me.

He thinks I'm right? He's arguing in my favor—in front of all that's left of our town?

Did he take a blow to the head in the middle of the destruction last night?

Then the comments being tossed around penetrate my consciousness.

Norbert the old cobbler is waving his hand toward me dismissively. "We can't trust anything that comes out of that girl's mouth. Even her own godlen didn't trust her enough to give her a gift."

The crouched figures nearby sway uneasily. A woman farther back is sniffling. "The Darium empire always wins."

One of the devouts who escaped the All-Giver's temple dips his head. "We took one of their lives, and they took our whole town. You can't conquer every foe."

I feel my aunt's piercing gaze on me before I pick out her face in the crowd. "Signy never could make anything of herself. She's the last person any of us should be following."

Jostein's bright blue eyes have fixed on me again. His mouth slants at a discomforted angle. "Your dedication sacrifice was rejected?"

A heaviness presses down on my chest. I force a tight smile, wiggling my remaining toes within my boots, not that he can see them. "I asked Inganne for more creative talent. Apparently she didn't think I'd make a good artist."

And what that has to do with my opinions on the Darium empire, I can't really see. But more disheartened mutters are still passing through the crowd, any rebellious energy that was left dwindling by the second.

Landric shakes his head, though his stance has already started to deflate as if he can tell this is a losing battle. "If Signy knows about anything, it's how to survive without much support. She pulled together an entire household with the scraps everyone else threw away."

"Because she couldn't manage better," someone calls out, and another burst of disparaging murmurs follows.

I suppress a wince and lower my head. The insults sting, but they're nothing new.

What prickles deeper is the frustration that's gripped me since the first moment I saw the Darium soldiers swing at Mom's fountain. The frustration that's maybe been simmering in me for longer than I knew.

How can they just give up? How can they shrug off the latest horror the Darium empire has inflicted on us on top of so many others?

The dukeling liked to call me the waif of refuse, but it's

all the rest of them who've been sitting down and eating a pile of shit without complaint, day after day. And now we're absolutely mired in it.

Unless we find a way to dig ourselves out. To throw the shit right back at the pricks who buried us in it.

What do any of us have left to lose? I've certainly got nothing.

I square my shoulders and lift my gaze again, pitching my voice to carry. "Just listen!"

I'm still a little surprised when the barrage of voices falls silent. Not knowing how long their grace will last, I hurtle onward. "We have a chance. Even the empire knows we do. The Darium soldiers must see our rebellion as a legitimate threat or they wouldn't have come down on us so harshly over one brief scuffle."

"Or maybe they're just bastards," someone grumbles.

"No," I say. "They're not used to anyone fighting back. It terrifies them. They've gotten complacent—because we've gotten complacent, just taking whatever they inflict on us. They aren't prepared for a real uprising. None of them have needed to face one before."

The soldier next to Jostein, the one with blond hair tucked behind his ears and a roguish grin, arches a skeptical eyebrow at me. "And you think you're in a position to face them? The entire Darium army?"

I stare steadily back at him. "Yes, I do."

My gaze travels over the townspeople hunched all through the woods around me. "If we strike out at them again, fast and effectively, while they're thinking they've cowed us, we could do some real damage. And the more we push back and tear them down, the more people from other towns will realize it's possible and join us."

The image unfurls in my mind's eye, the way I can sometimes look at a cracked bucket or a tattered net and see how it could be mended into something functional again. Veldunians standing up against Darium soldiers all across the country. Not just hundreds but tens of thousands of us, fueled by centuries of bottled anger.

My voice falters with the enormity of what I'm saying, but I push the words out. "We could… We could take our whole country back. If we're just willing to try."

Someone snorts, and someone else makes a scoffing sound. "That's dreaming too big."

But the image has taken hold of me too forcefully for me to back down. I can almost taste it, the freedom from fear and tyrannical demands. The knowledge that our home was really ours, with the rules and justice we decided on.

Where no child ever lost someone they loved because an asshole in a skeleton-painted uniform took offense.

"It's not," I insist. "Not if we show the rest of Velduny what's possible. There's—there's a Darium guard post just an hour's ride southeast of here. That's probably where some of the pricks who burned our town are holed up now, rejoicing their 'victory.' I say we burn the guard post down to the ground as payback. I'll go do it even if I have to by myself."

"And what would they do to us next?" Norbert demands.

I pause, and a laugh hitches out of me with the obvious answer. "What could they do? How would they even know who attacked them, or where to find us? They took away the place where we lived. Now all of Velduny is our home."

A burst of more emphatic conversation erupts, voices clashing and colliding, but a note of excitement reverberates through some of them.

They're listening. They're seeing what I see.

The captain steps in, her square jaw tight. I suppose I should be glad she hasn't brought out the gag she threatened yet.

She glowers at me. "All right, you said your piece. But

you're not burning anything down while you're tied to a tree. What your neighbors need is rest and healing, not a call to arms."

Jostein shifts his weight from one foot to the other and glances over at her. His expression has tensed even more than before. "Captain... She has made some good points. I think she could see them through."

As I clamp my teeth to avoid gaping at him in shock, his captain's head jerks toward him. I'm even more shocked that she doesn't snap at him for contradicting her but studies him pensively.

"Let's not hear any insubordination out of you, squad leader," she says, but her voice is simply terse, not outright cutting.

The blond man who seems to be Jostein's friend rocks back on his heels with an air of restless enthusiasm. "One little guard post, hit it in the middle of the night, no one the wiser... We *could* just see what happens. Baby steps rather than diving in headfirst."

The captain lets out a growl of irritation. "Iko, you can't call instigating war a 'baby step.'"

He shrugs and offers her one of his crooked grins. "I think I just did."

The captain glares at both him and Jostein for a moment. Then she points at me. "I think this one is stirring up enough trouble with her neighbors. You two, bring her over to my tent so she can't disturb them any more while we figure out what to do with all of these people. I trust between the two of you, you can keep her restrained."

She marches off through the trees. A hush has fallen over our makeshift camp.

An ache expands in my stomach. So now I'm going to be set apart from the rest of my town all over again, when we don't even have a town left?

Jostein and Iko exchange a look I can't read. Jostein crouches next to me to untie the rope that binds me to the tree trunk while Iko kneels by my ankles. I guess I should be glad they're going to let me walk rather than carting me over like a trussed pig.

They leave my wrists tied and yank me to my feet by my elbows. My legs wobble after so long sitting in that cramped position.

Landric is still on his feet. "You're not really going to—"

Jostein aims a hard look at him. "Captain's orders. No one's going to hurt your woman."

I sputter indignantly. "I'm not his."

Iko hums in apparent amusement and tugs me forward.

We tramp between the trees in silence, past a few small tents the soldiers have set up to a slightly taller one with a little Veldunian flag waving from its front post.

Inside, we find the captain sitting on a stool by the far end. She has a map unrolled on her lap.

At our entrance, she nods and makes a brief gesture for the men to sit me down across from her. They let go of me, Jostein a little warily. "Do you want us to bind her legs again? She does have a habit of running off."

The captain shakes her head. "I don't think that'll be necessary."

The men move to leave, but she clears her throat. "Actually, I'd like to speak to both of you too."

Something in her tone sharpens my attention. I peer at her as she sets the map aside and considers me in return.

Jostein and Iko stay where they are, Jostein's posture stiff with tension and Iko slinging his thumbs in his belt in a casual stance.

"You raised some interesting points," the captain says to me. "I see the guard post you mentioned. There wouldn't be more than ten soldiers stationed there at any given time, if that."

I shrug. "It'd be a start. A symbol that we can fight back."

"Or simple revenge."

My jaw clenches. "If I only wanted revenge, I'd have hunted them down years ago for killing my parents. I'm tired of standing back and letting them screw us over again and again. I'm tired of feeling like nothing we do matters, because they can step in and ruin it in an instant. Do *you* like pretending to have some authority when you're really just their puppet?"

A muscle ticks in the captain's cheek. She fixes her gaze on the men. "And you agree with the sedition she's spouting?"

Jostein manages to tense even more. "I can see the logic to her strategy, if someone *was* going to push back against the empire."

Iko snorts. "Let's not pretend that all of us wouldn't like to see all those Darium pricks with their heads on pikes."

"Hmm." The captain glances down at the map and back at us. "We're staying here another day while we gather supplies for these people and determine where they might be taken. So there would be plenty of opportunity for just a few of this company to slip off after dusk falls and put their words into action."

Jostein's eyes widen so much I think they might fall out of his head. "You're saying—"

"I'm saying if you believe in this one, you can stand with her—and fall with her. Stir up the makings of a rebellion if you can. If you're caught…" The captain lifts her shoulder. "I'll say you deserted our company and condemn you."

My breath catches in my throat. She's really agreeing to this plan.

But the men have far more to lose than I do. I look over at them, my heart pounding.

Iko nods, a subtler smile curving his lips. After a moment, with a flex of his jaw, Jostein does too.

"Someone has to light the first match," he says. "I couldn't ask anyone else to do it if I won't myself."

Iko gives a muted whoop and pumps his fist in the air. "Let's go hand those Darium bastards their asses!"

CHAPTER SIX

Signy

I wake up in the captain's tent to the thump of a bowl set down by my head. I jerk upright, my mouth tasting like sawdust, my eyes bleary.

I didn't mean to fall asleep. My exhaustion from the fraught, sleepless night must have caught up with me.

The captain sits on her stool by the little folding desk. "You'd better eat something before you go. I'd rather not have two skilled soldiers go down because you fainted with hunger in the middle of your rebellion."

I pull the bowl toward me. The meaty smell that wafts off it has my stomach gurgling in anticipation.

Starkly conscious of the captain's attention on me, I wolf the stew down as quickly as I can without looking like a total animal. As the gnawing of hunger subsides, curiosity tickles up in its place.

I consider her in the glow of the lantern. "Why are you letting us do this at all?"

"I don't believe you can win much of anything without

taking a few risks along the way. I just want to make sure they're the right risks before I invest very much in them."

She stands, collects my bowl, and sets a canteen down in its place. "Your parents were killed by Darium forces?"

I nod. She heard me say as much this morning.

Something hardens in the captain's eyes. "A couple of their soldiers killed my brother." She straightens up. "I imagine it won't be long before your companions come to collect you. No one will be on watch at this end of the camp, but try to be discreet about it, for my plausible deniability, please."

She ducks out of the tent without waiting for my response. But a reply doesn't really feel necessary.

We all have our reasons to hate the usurpers, don't we?

I take a gulp from the canteen to wash down the stew and take stock. The captain removed the rope around my wrists before I fell asleep. I'm wearing the same simple tunic and trousers I was yesterday, discards I patched up like I did my boots. I wouldn't have minded a dunk in a river and a change of clothes, but beggars can't be choosers.

My pocketknife remains nestled at my hip. It's hardly a fearsome weapon, but it's better than nothing.

I roll my shoulders and stretch my legs. Even if it was unintentional, I'm grateful for the sleep. Now that I've fully woken up and eaten, my thoughts are much clearer than they were this morning.

Is the mission I'm about to embark on insane? Possibly. But at least three people trained to know what a reasonable fight looks like seem to be on my side. So presumably it's not too crazy.

That doesn't mean I'm going to make it through the next five hours alive, but I still have nothing to lose.

I'd still rather die taking at least a few Darium soldiers down with me.

A whistle that sounds like a drunken bird sounds outside the tent, followed by a muffled mutter and a rustle of shifting clothes. The hushed voice rises just enough for me to make it out as Jostein's. "Signy?"

Swallowing hard, I ease aside the tent flap.

At first, I almost don't recognize the two men. Jostein and Iko have discarded their steel helms and burgundy soldier uniforms for plain shirts and trousers not all that different from mine.

They look more real somehow, like they're people I could actually know rather than distant figureheads.

Jostein waves me out with a small smile that sends an unexpected flutter through my chest. His now-visible rich brown hair, several shades darker than his bronze skin, only makes his blue eyes stand out more impressively.

The flutter only grows with Iko's soft chuckle. "I bet she would have figured out the birdsong just fine."

His hazel eyes gleam as they meet mine, his face even more roguishly handsome now that he's in clothes to match.

Gods smite me, I didn't quite notice before just how appealing both of these men are to look at.

I yank my mind back to the task at hand. "I'm here. Lead the way out of camp."

They'll have a better idea than I do which is the safest route to avoid notice.

As we slink between the trees, leaving the cluster of tents and my neighbors behind, I notice the swords sheathed at the men's hips are more modest too—short ones, only about the length of my forearm.

I guess typical military weaponry would draw more attention than we'd prefer. And also the captain wouldn't want any Darium forces who capture us to realize they've been attacked not just by Veldunians but specifically our local soldiers.

As the lantern light dwindles behind us, the men's strides lengthen. They pause in a small clearing, Jostein reaching into his pocket.

"It isn't much, but we thought you should be somewhat properly armed."

He hands me a curved hunting knife on its own leather strap that I can fasten around my waist. I draw the blade out for a moment to admire it in the hazy dusk. "I've never had a blade this nice."

Iko grins. "Nothing but the best for our rebel. Come—"

Footsteps rustle behind us, and we all stiffen. Before I can react with more than the lurch of my pulse, Landric hurries into view, his hands held up in a pose of surrender.

Jostein's hand leaps to his sword hilt. "What are you doing out here?"

Landric eyes the squad leader for a moment before his gaze slides to me. "You're going to the guard post like you talked about, aren't you? I could tell something was up, the way the captain pulled you aside."

I glare at him. "What's it to you?"

He blinks as if he's surprised I'm not celebrating his arrival. Sure, he stood up for me for about five seconds earlier today. Did he figure that somehow erased all the insults he and his friends have slung at me over the past several years?

Then he squares his shoulders, his annoyingly attractive face defiant. "I want to come with you. I want to help."

Jostein considers Landric with a skeptical expression. "It's going to be a long walk."

"That's fine. I'm ready."

Both of the soldiers shift their attention to me. Iko cocks his head. "Since this whole expedition was the lady's idea, I think the lady should make the final call."

Before I can open my mouth, Landric extends his hands toward me. "I'm sorry. The way things were around town—

none of it was fair to you. I think you're doing the right thing. Please, let me do something to help you this time."

I don't know whether I believe him, but my gut twists at the plea in his words. He pauses and then adds, "Even if you say no, I'll just follow behind you anyway. I know where you're going."

I let out a huff of breath and peer through the forest behind him. If we keep standing around, it's possible a sentry from the squadron will wander over this way and spot us.

Why shouldn't he put in a little work to offset the crap he's done in the past?

"Fine," I say brusquely. "Just make sure you keep up."

We set a swift pace through the woods and come out on the edge of a stretch of rolling hills. Moonlight glints off the peaks of the distant mountains.

Now that we're well clear of the camp, we veer in the actual direction of the guard post, which will bring us past Feldan. Our boots hiss through the long grass. Jostein peers up at the stars every few minutes, I assume making sure we stay on the right course.

After a long stretch of silence, too many thoughts are yammering in my head for me to stay quiet. I glance over at Landric. "What happened to your esteemed friends? Did they skip the celebration in town?"

I didn't see the dukeling or his noble sycophants among the survivors.

Landric shakes his head, his expression grim. "We came to the square, but Rupert and the others took off for their horses the second we heard the first call to evacuate."

"A more reasonable reaction than some others I'll refrain from mentioning," Jostein murmurs, but his tone is more dry than disparaging.

I glower at him. "It wasn't even their town, just a place near his dad's estate where he could slum it a little."

The soldier meets my gaze, the glint of his eyes sending another flutter through my pulse. "You were about to face an entire troop of Darium soldiers with nothing but a roasting spit. At least on this mission, the odds will be a little fairer."

My gaze slides back to Landric with the thought of another question I should ask. "What about your mother? Did she make it out?"

I haven't seen her, but then, I spent most of my time in the camp tied to a tree.

He releases a shaky breath. "Yes. She heard the calls and ran for the forest before the soldiers arrived. But I don't know how long it's going to take her to process the loss of all her inventory."

All the goods she would have traded or sold. I don't know what it's like to be a successful merchant—I have no idea what to say about that.

We lapse into a weightier silence for several minutes until Iko pipes up. "How does a dedicat to Inganne end up so warlike anyway? Shouldn't you be chasing butterflies and frolicking with paints?"

I roll my eyes at him. "I'd rather be making something beautiful than doing this. Or at least appreciating the beauty that's already there. The Darium empire just happens to be in the way."

I hesitate, but Landric already knows this. The soldiers might have heard it from my neighbors over the past day. It's not that much of a confession. "My mother was an artist. The statue they were destroying—it's one of her best pieces."

Or it was. I never got to even try to fix it before the assholes stormed the town.

The quiet that follows feels even heavier than before. Iko breaks it with the same breezy tone. "Of course, I'm not anyone to talk about odd dedications. How many soldiers do you meet who picked Estera to guide them?"

My gaze snaps to him. He dedicated himself to the godlen of wisdom and scholarship?

"Did you not expect to go into service back then?" I find myself asking, curious despite myself. Plenty of twelve-year-olds can't predict what course their lives will actually end up taking.

"Oh, I did. It was obvious the world needed a little more order, and I'm more than happy to provide—or attempt to, anyway. I just wanted to be smart about it." He winks at me.

Jostein speaks up, low but with a fond note that tells me they've been friends for quite a while. "His gift does come in handy for military operations sometimes."

Iko makes a dismissive sound. "It's only a small one. I was brave enough to march into battle but not to sacrifice more than a few patches of skin. A little extra inspiration for seeing how the things I have could be put to some new use. I have to work out all the finer details myself."

He nudges Jostein with his elbow. "This one's got all the ambition. Dedicated himself to Creaden."

I find I'm not surprised to imagine the stalwart squad leader being drawn to the godlen of authority, but he ducks his head as if embarrassed. "I haven't been able to see through that purpose very well so far."

"Hmph. You've got to make captain soon. Then major, then general, then why not rule the entire damned army?"

Jostein guffaws at his friend's irreverence. "We'll see."

I study him. I can't see any obvious dedication sacrifices on his body, but then, I can't see Iko's either. "Do you have a gift?"

It takes him a moment to answer, as if he needs to decide how to. "I have a knack for judging who can handle what tasks." His bright blue gaze slides to me. "That's the main reason I'm here. Every instinct Creaden gave me says you can see this mission through."

My heart skips a beat. He's sure I can do this—stick it to the Darium empire and survive? *I* wasn't even totally convinced.

But he believes it enough to have followed me on this perilous quest.

"You've accomplished a lot already," Jostein goes on, "even if I've given you a hard time about the risks you took. I'm not sure I've ever met a soldier as brave as you've proven yourself to be."

My skin flushes under his attention. I don't think any man has ever seemed this genuinely appreciative of me, let alone one as breathtaking as him.

I know what it's like to be lusted after. During my teen years, there were a couple of boys from town who managed to persuade me to let them get close... only to kick me aside after they'd gotten the itch out of their system, because of course the girl who was shunned even by her godlen wasn't worthy of anything but a rollabout or two. After the second time, I learned to keep my distance no matter what cajoling words a man murmured.

Jostein's interest doesn't feel anything like that. I don't know if he sees me as anything beyond a capable vigilante, but that's still more credit than anyone's given me in nearly a decade.

"I'll do my best to prove your instincts right," I find myself saying.

Iko flashes me another grin. "I have total faith in you too." He lifts his chin toward Landric. "What about you? Any hidden talents we should know about?"

I can't help wondering what my childhood playmate will say. Everyone in town talked about who dedicated to which of the lesser gods, so I know he picked Jurnus, but I don't remember hearing that he asked for a magical talent from the godlen of travel and communication.

Landric shakes his head. "There wasn't anything I could think of that I wanted enough to make the trade. Mostly I was hoping for Jurnus's guidance." He lets out a rough laugh. "I suppose he's giving me a good shove toward exploring the world now."

"The gods do work in mysterious ways. We have plenty of colleagues who forgo a divine exchange. After all, it's not as if a sacrifice is a guarantee."

Iko's voice halts abruptly with a darted glance toward me, his smile faltering. As if he's concerned that I'll be insulted by him touching on one of the most basic facts about my life.

I wait for someone to ask what I requested that Inganne judged as overreaching or why I think she denied me. Instead, there's only another silence more awkward than anything else.

Jostein adjusts our course so we can cross a stream at a rickety bridge. Reaching the dirt road on the other side, I kick aside lumps of dried horse dung that bounce into the grass.

We've given the town a wide berth, but a smoky scent taints the air even out here, even a day later. I squint, but I can't make out any of the landmarks amid the stretch of forest and jutting rocks that surround most of the town.

No temple spires. No memorial on the hill. They couldn't have burned the limestone, but it wouldn't have taken much to knock it down.

Are some of the other buildings still smoldering even now? Is there anything left it'd be worth returning for?

My little cabin might have gone untouched, set off from the rest of the town as it is, but the thought of living there next to the ruin makes my stomach roil.

The men have followed my gaze. Landric's jaw has

tightened, maybe thinking about his family's inventory turned to ashes or so damaged it may as well be.

Everyone from town will be starting over from scratch, but most have concrete skills they can quickly bring to bear. A merchant's talent for sales can't matter much without merchandise to peddle.

Iko wets his lips. I expect him to make some flippant remark to try to ease the tension, but instead his voice comes out cautious. "The way your neighbors talked about you—have they always been that harsh?"

Landric's expression twitches, but I don't see any point in dressing up the situation. "No. Not until I became a burden. I'd lost both my parents by the time I was eight, and my aunt and uncle weren't happy about taking me in. Then my dedication sacrifice was rejected, and no one wanted to associate with a girl even the gods had shunned. Wouldn't want the ill-favor to rub off on them."

Jostein frowns. "Just because you asked too much once doesn't mean the gods have rejected *you*."

I shrug. "Sometimes it seems like they did before I even made my sacrifice."

Iko's tone turns unexpectedly fierce. "Dariu has taken too many good people from this country. That's on them, not the gods."

I look at him, startled by his vehemence, and he grimaces as if in apology. "One of my good friends when I was growing up—we were running around in the street, and she tripped and bumped into a Darium soldier walking by. The prick yelled that she was a pickpocket and stabbed her before she could even get out an apology."

A chill wraps around my gut.

Jostein is nodding, his expression even more solemn than usual. "My uncle—he ran a tavern. A squadron came in and started harassing the barmaids. He and my cousin stepped in, and they murdered both of them."

Landric looks at the ground. "My father. Competition over a deal. Just greed."

I haven't thought about that in ages. As I look at him, my throat constricts. Maybe it makes sense that he insisted on coming on this mission after all.

I don't know if the Darium empire can ever repay everything they owe us, but they're going to make a small start tonight.

Chapter Seven

Signy

We stop well before we reach the glow of the guard post's lantern, which is hanging over the door of the wooden structure. A couple more lights glow in the second-floor windows.

I flex one calf and then the other. The walk took three peals of the hourly bells ringing in the temples and villages we've passed at a distance.

Jostein considers the terrain around the guard post. It's mostly open fields with a few low hills to the east and south, but a sparse woodland starts several paces to the north of the building.

He tips his head toward the trees. "Let's circle around, staying out of view, and see what we can make of the place from closer up."

We have to cross another road dotted with horse dung on the way over. None of us speaks, keeping our ears pricked for any hint of discovery by the soldiers inside the post.

We make it to the scattered trees without any calls of alarm. But then, even if a soldier on guard noticed a few figures walking across the nearby fields, they'd probably assume we're no threat.

When was the last time anyone truly challenged Darium authority?

We sneak between the trunks until we've come up alongside the building within the shelter of the trees. We're close enough that I can make out muffled voices and a brief chuckle but not most of the words.

Then someone who must be near an open window or in the upper lookout that's open to the air lets out a disgruntled sigh. "My uniform still smells like fucking smoke."

Her companion snorts. "That'll take ages to come out. At least you have happy memories to go with it."

"Happier if we could have barbequed all those stupid peasants."

"I wish I'd been able to join the razing. To see a bunch of ungrateful Veldunians crushed—can't get better than that."

My teeth set on edge. Ungrateful? What exactly do these assholes think we're supposed to be grateful for—the honor of having them shove us around and steal what's ours?

"Bastards," Landric growls under his breath.

Jostein's gaze looks even more determined than before. "How are we going to do this? I've got a flint, and all that wood will be flammable, but we've got to get the fire to the post before they can stop us. And make sure it'll spread quickly enough that they can't just stamp it out."

Iko hums to himself. "We should have brought some pitch. It burns like anything."

"I don't think Captain Amalia wanted us stopping to make supply runs along the way."

My mind trips back over our journey alongside memories of the odd sorts of kindling I've had to resort to at the worst of times. "We might have something just as good."

Jostein's eyebrows lift. "What?"

I aim a slanted smile at him. "Dried horse manure is almost perfect fuel if you don't mind the smell. And I'd say in this case that's a benefit rather than a downside. Especially if we mix it into balls with dead leaves or grass…"

I'm expecting the men to recoil, and maybe Landric does, but I'm paying the least attention to him. Jostein nods slowly, and Iko clasps his hands together with an air of excitement. "We can find plenty of that along the road. The summer heat will have baked it dry quickly—it hasn't rained for days."

"We still have to get the burning dung into the building," Landric points out. "I guess it'd be too heavy for arrows even if we had a bow… A strong enough throw might cross that distance."

Iko's face lights up. He reaches to one of the trees, just barely bigger than a sapling, and tugs on a pliant branch. "We don't need to risk falling short. It'd be easy enough to turn part of a tree into a miniature catapult."

Jostein chuckles. "Get to it then, master inventor. We'll collect all the fuel we can."

Without a word of complaint, Landric hustles alongside the squad leader and me back toward the road. He produces a sack of thin canvas that was folded in his pocket.

"You never know when you might see something worthy of collecting," he says at my surprised glance, with a hesitant grin.

I'm not going to reject his contribution. It'll beat hauling horse shit around in our arms.

We pick our way along the road, snatching up the harder, grittier droppings that are obviously older and tossing them into the bag. Wrinkling my nose, I grab a few pieces that are still partly damp as well. "To stick it all together."

When we head back through the trees, we all stop to pick up any fallen leaves that've turned crackly brown. I add the tiniest stray twigs I can find to the mix.

By the time we reach Iko, he's carved a branch as tall as he is off one of the trees and is testing its capabilities by launching rocks in the opposite direction from the guard post. He sends one flinging as high as the treetops just as we reach him and beams at us triumphantly. "Just need to trim a little more off the top, and it'll be perfect."

Jostein swipes his hands together. "I'll survey the site around the building again and pick the best position to launch from."

I hunker down next to the sack, and Landric follows suit across from me. "Looks like we're stuck with manure duty," he says.

I reach into the sack. "No one said you had to stick your hands into shit."

He replies steadily enough. "What am I here for if I'm not going to pitch in every way I can?"

A fair question.

He watches me shape the first ball, packing several droppings with leaves and twigs and a little damp manure to glue it all together. The final result is as big as a round of bread.

Copying my technique, Landric forms a couple of his own. In the end, we have enough for five projectiles.

Returning, Jostein appraises our work and motions us all over to the edge of the trees by the back corner of the guard post. "We'll want to fling them in there in quick succession, before they realize what's hit them. Here's the flint. I need to get to the door as soon as they start fleeing."

He flicks his fingers down his front in the gesture of the divinities and unsheathes his sword.

A sense of ominous anticipation grips me like nothing

I've ever experienced before. My heart is thudding, but I have the urge to yell some kind of war cry and pound my feet in a primitive dance.

We're really doing this. We're going to show these murderers what it's like to really have your lungs filled with smoke.

Landric takes the flint. I hold up the first globe of dung while he lights the spark to its side.

On the second try, the spark catches. I adjust my hands, waiting until the flames have crept all the way over one side of our projectile and dug deeper inside. Heat wafts over me, but it only spurs on the excitement quivering in my chest.

I place the flaming ball on the back of Iko's branch catapult. He shifts the angle slightly, braces himself, and lets it fly.

As the fiery dung ball careens through the air, I'm already holding out the second one to Landric. I only wait until I'm sure the fire has totally caught before yanking it over to Iko.

Shouts reverberate from the guard post. As Iko launches the second ball into the air, I'm vaguely aware of Jostein sprinting across the open ground between the trees and the building's walls. Most of my attention is on getting the rest of our projectiles lit.

It's only between the fourth and fifth that I let myself take the swiftest glance between the trees. My breath catches.

I drag my gaze back to the lump of dung and leaves I need to heft, but the flames flaring above the wooden walls and climbing to the lookout blaze on in my memory.

More yells ring out alongside the rising roar of the fire. Metal clangs, and bodies thump.

My heart stutters with the thought of the threats Jostein is facing alone, but all I can do is keep up my part of the bargain.

The instant Iko has propelled the final fiery dung ball

into the guard post, he drops his catapult, and we all run after Jostein. I whip my hunting knife from its sheath, not sure how to land the best blows but knowing I'll fight with everything I have regardless.

As my gaze catches on Jostein in the wavering glow of the fire, my rushing steps slow. He's just slamming his sword into the gut of one of the Darium soldiers, right where there must be a joint in the basic armor.

The enemy soldier crumples with a spurt of blood over his lips, next to four other foes Jostein has already toppled all on his own.

I guess a warrior has an advantage when they're prepared and their opponents are dashing around in a panic. All the same, he cuts a magnificent figure. I've never seen anyone wield a blade that skillfully.

One more soldier stumbles out of the flaming building. Iko springs forward to run him through.

The four of us remain braced around the guard post's entrance, but no one else hurtles toward us. Any other guards currently stationed there must have succumbed to the fire.

When it's obvious that no one could still be living inside the inferno that's baking my face, I take a step back and sheathe my knife. A victorious, giddy laugh tumbles out of me.

Iko whoops and slings his arm around me, spinning both of us around as if we're in the middle of a dance. "We did it. We destroyed those fuckers."

As he sets me back on my feet, his handsome face fills my entire view, his gray eyes glinting with delight. In that moment, I think he might kiss me.

I think I might want him to.

My pulse hiccups, and he lets me go.

As I wet my lips, the motion sending a tingle of desire

through me, Landric cranes his neck toward the far side of the fort. "They've got a stable. Maybe we can ride back."

The thrill of triumph sweeps through me again, strong enough to carry every other consideration away. The words spill out of me.

"There's a whole fort less than a day's ride north of here. Who says we have to stop now? Let's show Captain Amalia just how worthy this risk is."

The men stare at me for a moment. Then Jostein breaks into a soft laugh of his own.

Iko claps his hands, his teeth flashing in a feral grin. "I like the way you think, Spitfire. Let's ruin them all."

CHAPTER EIGHT

Signy

I f I'd known how big a Darium fort actually is, maybe I wouldn't have made such a bold suggestion.

I peer over the top of the knoll from where I'm sprawled in the grass, fidgeting with my sleeve. It's still stiff from the dunk we all took in the river we crossed this morning. I'm glad to have let the current sweep away the worst of the grime of travel, but the water's left all my clothes a little tight against my skin.

Or maybe that's just the tension winding through my body as I stare at the stone wall below.

Next to me, Iko swipes his hand across his mouth. "Well, we're not burning much of that place."

The two-story building beyond the wall is built of stone too. I worry at my lower lip. "I guess the floors are probably wood?"

On the other side of Iko, Jostein frowns. "We're going to need more than that to work with. We can't even get to the floors until we're inside."

With two guards posted by the gate, it's hard to figure how we're going to accomplish even the first part of that sequence. And what are we going to do once we're inside? There must be three or four times as many soldiers stationed in the fort as we faced at the guard post.

As much as I admired Jostein's skill with a sword, it seems a bit much to expect him to tackle a few dozen armed men by himself, especially when they won't be fleeing a rampaging fire. Even with Iko in the mix, we'll be overwhelmed.

I'm not reckless enough to think Landric and I will contribute much to the slaying part of the plan.

Iko adjusts his position, the side of his arm grazing mine. A tingle of heat races over my skin, sending me back to the moment last night when he embraced me.

"Maybe we just harass them," he says. "Hurl some crap at them and irritate them. We could get alcohol or lantern oil in that town down the road, put together some basic incendiary devices."

My stomach knots. "That won't make much of a point. If anything, it'll make us look weak—prove that we can't really harm them at any kind of larger fortress."

But maybe that's true. Maybe I should call this absurd mission off before we get into real trouble.

Captain Amalia only asked us to destroy the guard post. We pulled that off. She might be willing to encourage more of her soldiers to join our rebellion now, and Landric and I could appeal to our neighbors...

Of course, even with a force of a hundred, I'm not entirely sure how we'd do any damage to the fort. All they have to do is keep the door shut and pelt us with arrows from above.

Was I out of my mind to think we could make a real stand against the Darium forces?

As my doubts gnaw at me, a large horse-drawn cart

comes rattling along the road at the base of the hill, which leads east from the nearby town past the fort. I expect it to continue on by, but instead it veers onto the side lane to the fort's gate.

At my other side, with a careful distance between us, Landric makes a thoughtful sound. "Of course. They'd have a merchant from town bringing supplies regularly. They never bother with any grunt work they can make one of us do for them."

It appears he's right. The cart comes to a stop in front of the gate, and the driver waits while one of the guards scans the cargo: lumpy burlap sacks, casks of ale, a couple of baskets of fruit.

The guard steps back with his arms crossed over his chest. His brusque voice carries up the hill. "Commandant Paulo wants more of that pork roast tomorrow. And it'd better be fresher this time."

The merchant bobs his head with obvious anxiety and murmurs something obsequious. The other guard pushes open the door and ushers in the cart.

Landric leans his chin on his folded hands. "That's one way to get inside."

Jostein knits his brow. "We couldn't hide on that thing without the driver noticing us. He'd need to agree to the scheme."

"I can't imagine he likes his employers all that much," I say.

"He probably likes not being slain by them." Jostein tips his head to the side. "Let's head over to town so we can at least find out where he's coming from."

"And grab ourselves something to eat," Iko puts in. "I'm starving."

My stomach gurgles in agreement. We found a patch of

wild raspberry bushes on our trek, but the relief that snack brought has long since faded.

We tramp down the far side of the hill to the spot where we left the horses to graze. As Jostein helps me into the saddle and then swings up behind me, I will down the flush that creeps into my cheeks.

There were only three animals in the stable by the guard post. It makes sense that I'd be the one to double up, since I weigh the least, and he was the only one confident in handling the horse with a passenger in front.

I lean tentatively against his broad chest, doing my best not to think about the warmth of his muscular thighs on either side of mine. His arms wrap loosely around me, almost a hug, as he flicks the reins.

I'm already getting tingles when I'm close to Iko. Panting after both of them seems a bit much.

And then there's Landric, glancing over at us with a tightening of his mouth as if he's not entirely happy seeing me in another man's arms. The All-Giver only knows what's going on in his head.

I do my best to focus on the terrain around us and staying balanced as we trot across the fields, taking an indirect route toward the town so we aren't seen from the fort. I've only had the chance to ride a few times as a kid, many years ago. I forgot how unnerving being perched on a creature that has a mind of its own could be.

Jostein guides the stallion with total confidence, clicking his tongue so it perks its ears and steps a little faster. I turn my head so I can see his face at the edge of my vision. "You seem like you have a lot of experience with horses. Are you normally with the cavalry?"

Most of his colleagues who joined us once we met up with the captain were on foot.

He shakes his head, his chin grazing my hair. "My parents are horse breeders and trainers. I grew up with them. So my superior officers tend to give any riding-related tasks to me."

"All the better for him to sweep pretty ladies off their feet," Iko pipes up.

My cheeks outright flare, but Jostein simply snorts. "Or drag them away from disaster."

I decide I'm better off keeping my mouth shut for the rest of the ride.

Not far from the first buildings of town, we pass a wagon that's sagging amid the grass. One of the wheels has cracked through. Dirt stains the canvas covering on either side of a massive tear. I peer inside but find it empty. It looks like the owner must have taken out their cargo and abandoned it as unsalvageable, months if not years ago.

Because of our roundabout route, we circle around to the road just as the merchant's cart is returning to the town. We tie the horses at a hitching post on the main street and amble along at a cautious distance until we see him guide it around back of a grocer's shop a few streets beyond the central square.

The four of us wander into the shop as if just there to stock up on provisions. As Jostein and Iko pick out apples and eggs and a couple bottles of milk, voices filter from the back room—the merchant and his wife, I suspect.

"The delivery went smoothly?" she asks.

"No trouble at all. I'll just need to speak to the butcher tonight. As long as we keep them happy up there at the fort, we've nothing to worry about."

I find myself exchanging a glance with Landric. That attitude doesn't bode well for convincing him to turn on the soldiers.

Iko's faint grimace suggests he's drawn the same conclusion. He and Jostein pay the clerk for our selections, and we duck back out, gnawing on the apples and passing around one of the bottles.

The cool creaminess of the milk takes the edge off my hunger but doesn't lift my spirits. "Now what?"

Jostein sighs. "Let's go back to the square and get ourselves some bread from the bakery. It'll be easier to think once we've had a full meal."

Iko nods. "We should stroll around and visit each of the shops. You never know what else we might hear from the locals."

It's a nice thought, but we pass the last two hours of the afternoon gulping down our meager meal and overhearing nothing but basic pleasantries and irrelevant gossip between the townspeople. As evening sets in, Jostein checks his purse and declares that we have enough funds to splurge on a hot dinner at the tavern.

As we step into the loud, hazy space, my stomach sinks. I can't help thinking this is a gesture of condolence—that we'll eat and then the responsible soldier will declare that there's nothing more we can do here, that we need to head back to his squadron.

I'm not even sure what I could say in argument.

So I pick at my leg of roast chicken slowly at our table in the corner, peering at the customers around us as I chew. I almost choke on my current mouthful when three Darium soldiers push into the room.

They're wearing their standard uniforms, black with white bones, but no helmets, which only makes them slightly less terrifying. The locals at the nearby tables tense at their arrival, a few cringing to the side.

The man at the lead calls for mugs of ale without any

indication he's going to pay for them. The barkeep hustles to pour the drinks.

I can't help remembering Jostein's story about the soldiers who murdered his uncle and cousin.

One of the other soldiers waves her arm at the patrons already sitting at a prime table. They clutch their drinks and dash off to a more cramped one that remains open near the wall.

The previous bar chatter has dwindled. As the soldiers drop into their chairs and enjoy their drinks, the conversations only continue in lowered voices.

I force down my mouthful of chicken, my chest constricting. At least it doesn't seem the soldiers are here to investigate a recent guard post burning.

Landric shifts uneasily in his chair. He speaks under his breath. "Should we go?"

Jostein shakes his head, his voice pitched equally low. "It'll be noticeable, so soon after they arrived. Signy's only halfway through her dinner. We wait a little and then go."

I start plowing through my chicken at a much more enthusiastic pace.

I'm nearly down to the bone when a man gets up from a table a couple over from the soldiers'. His flushed face and unsteady balance suggest he's had a little more ale than is wise.

Especially in present company. He heads toward the bar, sways on his feet, and jostles the back of one of the soldiers' chairs.

The man jerks around with a snap. "Watch yourself!"

Then the woman who claimed the table lets out a chuckle that sends a shiver down my spine. "Thaddeus wanted to have more of a lark. Why don't you play darts with this one?"

I don't understand what she means until the soldier who

ordered the drinks gets to his feet. The drunk mumbles an apology, but the other man ushers him over to a dart board hanging on the side wall. "You disrupted our fun, you can help us have a little more."

"Thaddeus," his other colleague says with a trace of dismay, but he shuts his mouth when the larger man glares at him.

The drunk's friends still sitting at his table watch with paling faces, but no one else dares even try to intervene. The soldier positions the drunk right in front of the dart board. "Let's see how well I can outline that fat head of yours."

As he steps back with a handful of darts, my stomach churns. Jostein's shoulders stiffen, but Iko sets a hand on his forearm to warn him to stay put.

We could take down these three soldiers, but what would that mean for the town? Would we leave another smoking wreckage in the wake of our attempted rebellion?

We weren't prepared for this.

The soldier whips his first dart toward the drunk. It thuds into the wall less than an inch above his victim's rumpled hair. His friend gives a whoop of approval. The other soldier stares at his drink without a word.

So it continues, one dart after another, flying so close to the drunk's head he must feel the air shudder with their passing. The fourth dart hits a little too close, nicking the shell of his ear and falling to the floor.

The drunk gives a muffled yelp. Blood beads on his ear, but he holds himself even more still with a brief shudder.

The whole tavern has gone silent except for the soldiers. We watch as the last two darts smack the wood on either side of the man's neck.

"An enjoyable jape," the soldier says casually, and saunters over to pull out the darts. My hands clench at the thought that he might pick up the game all over again, but instead he shoves the drunk toward his table. "Keep your ass in your seat, and we shouldn't have any problems."

My gaze slides to the drunk's friends. Their sallow faces tighten with restrained anger as they track the soldier's assured stride back to his own chair.

An idea starts to come together in my head. There are a lot of things broken here... and we might not be the only people interested in fixing them.

It was never supposed to be only about us, after all.

I glance around at my companions, speaking at barely a whisper. "I think I see an opportunity here."

A small smile crosses Iko's face.

Jostein hesitates, but maybe his gift tells him I know what I'm talking about. "Give it your best shot."

At least one of us has faith in me. I'm not convinced yet that my conviction isn't just willful stubbornness.

The soldiers don't head out until after the next peal of the town bell. I wait another few minutes to be sure they aren't going to barge back in, but then I see the drunk and his friends getting up from their table.

I beckon my companions to follow me and hurry after them.

We catch up in the square just outside the tavern. Even the drunken man is walking fairly steadily, the encounter with the darts having sobered him up.

I come up beside them and clear my throat. "That was a sick game they played in there."

The four men slow, the main target of the soldier's game touching his blood-dappled ear.

"It is what it is," one of them says warily.

"But does it really have to be? There's more of us than there are of them."

Another of the bunch considers me with narrowed eyes. "What are you saying?"

I hold up my hands in a gesture of innocence. "Just speculating. It's been hard not to, lately... I don't know if you heard, but a group of Veldunian rebels burned down a Darium guard post just south of here last night. They took out all the soldiers who were in it."

I'm prepared to drop the subject there, but interest immediately lights in all four pairs of eyes, as much as the skeptic tries to keep a poker face.

"Serves them right," the third man mutters, and the skeptical one elbows him.

The drunk exhales roughly. "It does. I wouldn't mind seeing something like that here." Then his gaze darts around as if he's afraid the soldiers might be listening in.

"We're not doing anything with the fort right there," the skeptic grumbles.

I offer them a crooked smile. "Maybe you can, though. Word's being passed around between people who'd want to see some change. Anyone who'd like for the Darium army to get what they deserve should meet in the field west of town tomorrow at the tenth bell."

If we make it sound like someone else is organizing the scheme, the locals won't point us out as the instigators if they decide to tattle.

The men scan both me and the three men behind me. "You're all going?"

Iko joins in with a casual shrug, playing along with my story. "Might as well find out what could happen, right? No commitment."

The group exchanges glances. I step back as if I'm not all that invested. "I just thought you might want a part in that. Don't pass on the word to anyone else unless you're sure they're more loyal to Velduny than the invaders."

The men walk on, murmuring amongst themselves, and we draw back into the shadows next to the tavern. The corners of Jostein's mouth have quirked upward. "What are you up to now, rebel maiden?"

I ignore the giddy quiver the nickname sends over my skin and rub my hands together. "I've got a wagon to fix, and then we'll need to do some more grocery shopping."

CHAPTER NINE

Iko

The pungent chemical smell of lantern oil wafts out of the bottle. Wrinkling my nose, I stuff the last rag partway down the neck and watch the liquid gradually saturate it.

Signy straightens up from where she was crouched by the side of the old wagon. Her movement, all athletic grace, draws my gaze automatically.

She pats the side of the wagon, which is now standing evenly on four solid wheels and stripped of its ragged covering. "There. All we need to do is harness the horse and load it up."

I leap to my feet. "I'll help you with that. I think we've got a good supply of explosives now."

Signy eyes the rows of assembled bottles and lets out a soft laugh. "I should probably be worried by how much you seemed to enjoy putting those together."

I thought she was pretty from the first moment I saw her

hollering for her neighbors to push back the Darium soldiers, but when she smiles, my heart skips a beat.

I grin back at her. "Who doesn't enjoy a good blast?"

As she fiddles with the harness, a mix of the abandoned one that'd started to rot and fresh strips of leather we scavenged from the shoe shop's rubbish heap, I lead over the largest of our three stolen stallions. It's obvious that this woman has never harnessed a horse before, so she lets me take the lead, eyeing the animal warily. But despite her uncertainty, she rises to the task with the same unshakeable determination I've seen over and over in the past few days.

How did this incredible woman manage to drop into my life out of nowhere, in the worst of circumstances?

We heave the three large casks we've acquired into the front of the cart. I check to confirm that the lid will easily pop off before stocking the base of each with several doctored bottles and a flint. Signy should fit inside easily enough, but it'll be more of a squeeze for any of the rest of us.

As we load up the rest of the crates and sacks, mostly stuffed with trash with only a topping of food showing where necessary to sell the story, Jostein and Landric come riding over on the other two horses.

Jostein hefts the raw roast in its waxed paper wrapping and nestles it in clear view. It's the key to our entry to the fort after all.

Landric dispenses handfuls of battered fruits and vegetables from his sack, carefully arranging them so only the best parts are showing. He motions to Signy. "I got your lemons!"

I can't help watching the interplay of emotions on his pale face as she hustles over to collect the yellow fruit. He's trying to play it cool, but there's an almost desperate intensity to his gaze.

I don't think she notices how much it bothers him that

she's still standoffish with him. And I suspect that bothers him even more.

But if he used to talk to her the way the rest of her idiot neighbors did the other morning, her aloofness serves him right.

Signy gets down to work cutting into the lemons and squeezing juice into a few small oilskin pouches. Before I can ask her what she's planning on seasoning with the stuff, Jostein grunts in warning.

Several figures are heading our way from town. I hop up on the back of the cart for a better view. "They're all wearing regular clothes, no soldier uniforms. Three of them are from the bunch we talked to last night, a couple of women around the same age, and two older men. I think they're all right."

I don't have any magical gift for judging people's intentions, but the grim resolve I can make out on the new arrivals' faces and the forcefulness of their strides suggests they're committed to a task they expect to be risky but worthwhile. If they were coming out here just to betray us, I'd expect to see more nerves or signs of guilt.

We all gather together to meet our accomplices. As they near, I take in the details with a growing sense of satisfaction.

Not only do they look resolved, they've also come prepared. The two older men are carrying crossbows, as is one of the younger men. One of the women has a regular bow slung over one shoulder and a quiver of arrows on the other. The other woman and two men carry hunting knives.

They're definitely anticipating a battle.

I step a little ahead of my companions and smile in welcome. "Good to see you all here. Are you ready to crack some Darium heads?"

A gleam comes into the eyes of one of the younger men. "Are we taking them on today? Where are we going at them?"

The older man next to him gives him a nudge. "I'd like to

know who we're dealing with first, Sepp—and they'll want to know who we are."

Sepp ducks his head with an abashed look. "We were careful, like you said. This is my dad and a friend of his, Otmar. They do a lot of hunting—they know how to handle a weapon. And Tilman and Weiland brought their wives. The more of us can pitch in, the better, right?"

Jostein considers the group. "What happened to your other friend from last night?"

It's the drunken one who's missing, the one the soldier aimed his darts at.

Tilman grimaces. "He's too hungover to be much use this morning, and I'm not sure he'd have the guts for it anyway. But those pricks from the fort have been terrorizing the whole town for too long. If we can do something about it..."

Otmar the hunter adjusts his crossbow under his arm. "What *are* we going to do? Who called for this expedition?"

Before I can speak, Signy spreads her hands apologetically. "It's just us. Last night, we needed to be careful too. But we've already destroyed one of their guard posts, just the four of us. With a little more strategy and the seven of you, I think we can take down the entire fort." She tips her head toward the distant building.

"Who *are* you?" Sepp's father demands, though his face has lit up at the promise of her suggestion.

Landric motions between him and Signy. "Darium soldiers destroyed our home a few days ago. We've had enough. It's time to send the invaders running."

Weiland's wife eases closer to the cart. "What exactly is the plan? We can't all fit in the cart."

My mind has already been spinning through the possibilities, but Jostein is the most natural leader among us. He probably took stock before they even introduced themselves.

He points to the casks. "We can have three people hiding in the barrels—they're empty. The women are the smallest, so I'd suggest the three of you for that task. Iko will drive the cart, since he's the best at bullshitting his way through tense situations." He shoots me a wry smile.

"Guilty as charged." I salute him and then turn to our new allies. "I've stocked the casks with several homemade incendiary devices and flints. You'll have about ten seconds from when you light the rags to throw them before the glass bursts on you. I'll signal you when it's time—I'll stop the cart partway through the door and say, 'I almost forgot something.'"

Signy points to the one woman's bow. "You can stash that and your arrows between the sacks and grab them when you need them. And we also have these." She hands over the pouches of lemon juice and tosses the last to me. "Throw it in the soldiers' faces when they get close. It'll blind them for a little while."

Clever as well as brave. I attach the pouch to my belt. "The three of you can use the casks as shelter for as long as the situation allows. Just keep lighting and tossing out the bottles—the more fire and smoke we can get going, the more confusion there'll be that works to our advantage."

Jostein walks over to the horses. "As soon as we see the first spurts of fire, the rest of us will charge in from over the nearest hill. I'll ride... and it'd be good to have someone else particularly skilled with arms at the front of the charge." He beckons Otmar over. "Landric will lead everyone else on foot. Just get in there as quickly as you can and stop any soldiers who try to run or ride off. Any concerns?"

The newcomers have gone wide-eyed, taking it all in, but I can tell it's as much excitement as anxiety flushing their faces. Jostein sounds so confident I already believe we'll pull the whole plan off without a hitch.

Signy leaps into the cart, her eyes glinting fiercely. "They won't be expecting a thing. They figure they've got us all cowed. We're about to show them different."

Her words propel everyone into action. Otmar strides over to join Jostein at the horses.

Landric motions for the other men to follow him. "Come on, we need to get going to make sure we're in position ahead of the cart."

They set off at a brisk tramp, and Signy and I help the two women into the cart. They slide tentatively into the barrels, their feet setting the bottles clinking quietly, and crouch down.

"You've found the flints?" I check. "We jabbed a few discreet air holes so you should be able to breathe just fine, and the lid will pop off the moment you smack it. Let's try it just so you know how it'll feel."

Signy ducks down into her own cask, and they practice a couple of bursts out of hiding. By the second time, the other women are laughing breathlessly.

"It's really going to work," one of them says.

I smirk. "The assholes aren't going to know what hit them."

With the lids in place, I take my seat at the front of the cart. I touch the blanket I laid there, which is covering the new weapon I spent a few hours last night constructing after a flare of gift-given inspiration, and then twitch the reins.

The stallion heaves forward, and the abandoned wagon rolls after him.

Even with our mostly false load, it's enough of a burden that our pace is about the same as if we were walking. I expect we've given Landric and his followers a solid enough lead that they'll be in place in time even with their roundabout route.

Jostein really was quite astute in how he divided us up.

Every group has at least one of our original four in it, so our new allies won't be unsupervised.

As I direct the horse onto the lane that leads to the fort, I glance toward the nearby hill. A flash of black cloth atop it confirms that the others are ready.

But this next step depends entirely on me.

I keep my posture straight as the horse clops up to the gate and draw the cart to a stop a few paces away. The two guards posted outside peer at me with vaguely puzzled expressions.

"Xaver fell off a ladder and broke his arm last night," I say, using the name I gathered with a little chatting around town. "He sent me instead. Wanted to get that pork roast to your commandant bright and early."

I motion to the hunk of meat, dribbling a bit of blood through the folds of the paper.

One of the guards walks over and then nods. "Thank you. He'll be glad to hear it."

They move to open the gate.

No expression of condolences for the grocer's supposed injury, but I didn't expect one. And barely a hint of caution.

How very complacent they've gotten. So sure every Veldunian is too beaten down to stand against them.

I'm looking forward to proving how wrong they are.

The gate creaks open. I tap the horse forward. The cart's wheels crunch over the pebbles embedded in the dirt.

When we're as far inside as we can get while still blocking the gate from shutting, I tug the stallion to an abrupt stop. My pulse thunders, but I manage to say the words loud and clear.

"I almost forgot something."

I yank my doctored weapon out from under the blanket and spring to my feet. In the few seconds it'll have taken for the women to light their first rags, I've aimed the morphed crossbow at the guards by the gate and shot three arrows with one press of the trigger.

One of the men was already starting to duck. The arrow pierces the center of his forehead. The second flies wild, but the third strikes the other guard in the chest.

Then the women erupt from the casks, and flames streak through the air.

Amid the shattering of glass on the hardened earth, shouts ring out all through the fort. I jump into the shelter of the cart and jam three more arrows into my bow.

More bottles careen through the air. Flames roar up from the splotches of spilled lantern oil. The tangy smoke prickles in my lungs.

The second the women duck into their casks again, I fire off another round of arrows toward the men rushing from the fort's main doorway.

All three hit their mark this time, though two are hardly fatal injuries. More soldiers are hurtling toward us.

I draw my sword instead and vault over the side of the cart.

Another round of bottles with burning rags smash to the ground, one setting a soldier's pantleg on fire. I swing my sword across another man's throat before he can get close enough to stab at Signy.

The woman who brought her bow hurls one last bottle and scrambles out to retrieve her weapon. She bobs in and out of shelter, firing at the approaching soldiers.

My sword clangs against a longer one. I shove my attacker backward with a kick to the gut.

And Jostein barrels through the gate with a thunder of hoofbeats, his own sword flashing through the air.

He cuts down two Darium soldiers in quick succession. Otmar gallops in right behind him, shooting from his single but totally acceptable crossbow.

At the corner of my eye, Signy clambers out of her cask and leaps right over the front of the cart.

With a lurch of my pulse, I spin around. She's already darting between the patches of flames, two more burning bottles in her hands.

She ducks under the sweep of a soldier's dagger and flings her cargo through the open door of the fort.

Toward the wooden floors.

Fire roars up within the building. Within seconds, the shouts take on a frantic edge.

I spring forward and grab Signy's arm, throwing myself between her and an attacker. As our blades clash, she whips out her hunting knife and rams it into the Darium soldier's gut.

When she steps back, it's not just exhilaration but pride shining in her face.

The fort is falling into ruin around us, and it's all because of her. She *should* be fucking proud.

Gods know I'm proud to have been here with her, making the triumph she envisioned real.

Jostein lets out a menacing yell and topples another foe. His stance radiates power and passion—all that fire our superiors have liked to claim he lacks.

Maybe my friend needed this rebellion just as much as Signy did.

With a barrage of thudding feet, the last of our number charges into the fort. Knives flash, and the older man adds his crossbow arrows to the projectiles soaring through the air.

A Darium archer from a high window risks shooting into the melee and carves a bloody line through Landric's bicep. The man barely flinches—and then Otmar has launched his own arrow straight into the enemy's throat.

I don't know how many we've already felled. I keep

slashing and stabbing while the fire crackles through the fort, until flames lick at the second-floor windows.

All at once, I realize the onslaught has stopped. There's no one around me except my co-conspirators.

We wait for a minute, our chests heaving with the exertion, our breaths rasping from the smoke. Then a triumphant laugh bursts from one of the women's throats.

She raises her fist in the air. "For Barba!"

Sepp imitates her gesture. "And for Krissem!"

Jostein's jaw tightens. "For Dirk and Fritzi!"

A lump clogs my throat. I propel the words past it. "For Lutza!"

For the first time, I really do feel like I've taken back some of the power Dariu has stolen from us for so long. Dealt back some of the horror they've inflicted on us for centuries.

We withdraw from the wreckage of the fort on shaky legs. Otmar dismounts to hand his horse over to me. He presses his arm against his side, where blood is seeping through his shirt.

"Just a scratch," he protests when his friends exclaim and hurry to bandage it. "More than worth it."

He turns to Sepp and his father. "We shouldn't let it stop here. Gods smite them all, we need them right out of our country. If we could manage this with just eleven of us…"

Sepp's father nods. "We'll go to Vadan and see who we can rally."

The woman with the bow taps her husband. "We could go to Childeric and do the same. We have to spread the word that the assholes can be beaten."

I grin at their enthusiasm, but Jostein looks abruptly concerned. "Spread the word," he says, "but lay low for now. If all goes well, the Veldunian army will mobilize in our favor. When our soldiers come to help you, you'll be able to do so much more damage."

With the elation emanating from our newly turned rebels, I'm not sure they'll listen to his caution. But then, I'm not even sure they should.

We don't waste time clearing out from the area of the fort and heading our separate ways. There's no evidence left behind to indicate who was responsible for razing the fort.

As far as the Darium empire is concerned, it might as well be all of Velduny. That seems fitting.

Our band of four rides south for most of the day, back toward Feldan where we can regroup with our squadron. We stop only to rest, graze the horses, and to wash off the worst of the battle grime at a pond. After the latter, I find a small clearing in the forest where I can let the sunlight bake some of the dampness from my hair and shirt.

Jostein follows me there. He swipes his dark hair back from his forehead and leans against the tree opposite me.

His gaze slides back in the direction of the stream, where we left Signy still washing to offer her some privacy. "She's really something, isn't she?"

There's more than awe in his voice. As I sit up straighter, a prickling sensation runs through my gut. "She is. I don't think I've ever met a woman like that."

My friend's attention returns to me, his bright eyes evaluating. "You've certainly dallied with enough of them before tossing them aside. She deserves better treatment than that, Iko."

I bristle at his implication. "There's a difference between two people knowing it was never anything worth keeping and 'tossing aside' someone. I hadn't met anyone I wanted more than that with."

An edge creeps into his voice. "But you have now?"

I narrow my eyes at him. "Have *you*? Since when do you let yourself get distracted by a pretty face?"

Jostein lets out a rough guffaw. "She's leagues more than that, which you know as well as I do. Gods smite me, I've never gotten in your way. You can't give me a chance the one time I want it?"

I push to my feet, the prickling heat that's a mix of anger and jealousy spreading up through my chest. "It's hardly up to either of us, is it? I'm pretty sure she's the sole decider of who she'd end up kissing and whatever else. And she should know what her options are."

Jostein's shoulders tense. "Iko—"

At the crunch of footsteps in the brush, we both jerk around.

Signy stops a few paces from the clearing. Her arms wrap loosely around her chest as if she needs the reassurance of an embrace. "What are you two talking about over here?"

CHAPTER TEN

Signy

I don't think I've ever seen Iko look remotely flustered before, but his tan face reddens as he seems to grope for the words to answer my question. My stomach drops.

All I made out of their low voices was something about "she" needing to know what her options are. And the only "she" around here is me.

What options could there be beyond heading back to their squadron and seeing how much farther we can take this mission? Are they discussing whether they should try to convince me to back down?

Why would they be having any kind of conversation that concerns me off where I can't be a part of it?

Iko opens his mouth to speak, but Jostein beats him to the punch. Though the squad leader looks a tad ruffled himself, his voice comes out with typical steadiness. "I mentioned to Iko how much I admire you, and he's trying to persuade me that I shouldn't act on my interest."

Even as my heart stutters at the confession, Iko is jumping in, his cheeks still flushed. "That wasn't it at all, Jos, and you know it. I was only saying that I have just as much right to express my own interest."

My jaw has gone slack. I glance from one handsome face to the other, my pulse recovered and thumping at twice as rapid a pace as usual. "You mean… You would want… *Both* of you…"

I can't quite seem to sort my thoughts out into a coherent order. I thought the flares of attraction I've felt were mostly if not entirely on my side.

I'm a nobody who's accomplished nothing before the last few days, whose own godlen didn't believe in her. How is it possible that not one but two stunning, capable men could want to court me?

"It's out there now," Jostein says to Iko, and turns his attention back to me. The intensity of his bright blue eyes sends a thrill down the middle of my chest. "You're the most incredible woman I've ever met, and I'd be honored to become more than just your colleague."

Iko rolls his eyes as if exasperated by his friend's formal phrasing. When he looks at me, there's something oddly nervous about his usual carefree smile. "You're fucking fantastic. I'd welcome the chance to give you everything you deserve from a man."

He pauses, taking in my reaction. "Although naturally you don't have to accept either proposition. If you're not inclined to be kissing either of us, we wouldn't press the issue."

A startled laugh tumbles out of me. I rake my hand back through my travel-mussed hair, my head still spinning, and look down at my feet. "That isn't the problem. I never expected… I think you're both incredible too."

There's a beat of silence, and then Iko cracks a grin. "We've made a good impression then."

"I guess you could say that," I mutter, and inhale slowly.

I've stared down Darium soldiers, ready to meet my death by their hands. I should be able to look these two men in the face while I'm talking about a much more enjoyable outcome.

I lift my eyes, girding myself. A blush tickles across my cheeks at the avidness in both their gazes. My heart is still thumping along far too quickly.

"We've only just started to get to know each other," I say. "I like both of you a lot so far. I don't think I could choose between you right now." Not without risking regretting that choice before long.

Gods above, how did I end up in the position to need to choose at all?

Iko cocks his head, his smile turning sly in a way that sets off sparks over my skin. "Maybe that's not a problem. You could get to know us both a little more at the same time." He glances at Jostein. "Friends don't have to pitch a fit about sharing, do they?"

Jostein blinks at him and then considers me. A glimmer of passion lights in his eyes. "We do work well together in many other ways…"

"Mmhm. So why not give this a try? Fan our spitfire's flames twice over."

Iko trails his hand down my arm, and I sway toward him automatically. Heat courses through my body, muddling my thoughts even more.

The soldier steps closer, brushing my hair back over my shoulder, and presses a tentative kiss to the side of my neck.

The graze of his lips brings a gasp to my throat. I tilt my head farther to offer him better access, my skin lighting up all the way down to my toes.

I haven't been touched with any kind of desire in more than two years. I'd forgotten how good it can feel.

It's *never* felt this good, with the certainty that the man offering it truly wants me for more than just his satisfaction.

As Iko deepens his attentions with a flick of his tongue, a strangled sound escapes Jostein. He eases in at my other side, tips my chin upward, and captures my mouth.

Great God help me, this is another realm of pleasure altogether. I kiss him back instinctively, more heat flooding my body and pooling between my thighs.

The two men enfold me, Iko teasing his hand across my belly to rest on my hip, Jostein caressing the small of my back. When Jostein releases my mouth to trail his lips along my jaw and nip my earlobe, Iko wastes no time in claiming a kiss of his own.

A whimper of need escapes me, which might be embarrassing if these men didn't seem to need me just as much.

Jostein stifles a groan and nibbles a path right down to my shoulder. His stroking fingers creep up under the hem of my skirt, drawing scorching lines on the bare skin of my back.

Not to be outdone, Iko lifts his hand to skim his knuckles over the peak of my breast through my shirt. My nipple pebbles with a jolt of bliss, and he swallows my gasp with the deepening of his kiss.

I grip his shirt and Jostein's arm, my legs abruptly wobbly. All at once I'm wondering whether I should *ever* have to choose.

Their combined attention is so delicious. How could anyone give this up once they've had it?

Jostein lets out a little growl that seems to demand he resume his claim on my lips. Iko draws slightly back with a soft chuckle—

And a twig cracks beyond the clearing with a rough inhalation.

All our heads snap around. Landric has halted several paces away into the forest, but well within view of our intimate embrace. His eyes have gone wide, his face wan but spotting with uncomfortable red before my eyes.

"I— Never mind." He whips around and strides away, his shoulders hunching.

A different sort of heat ripples through me—a mix of shame and anger that this man who's never treated me as better than trash before the past few days can make me feel that shame.

What's it to him who I kiss or how many?

Then it occurs to me with a sudden chill that my private choices might become much less private as soon as we reunite with our neighbors. Is he going to tell all of them that I've become some kind of insatiable seductress on top of all my other failings?

My stance tenses, the desire that consumed me earlier snuffing out.

Jostein sighs. "He'll get over it."

What's there to get over? It's not as if Landric's ever wanted me for himself.

I shake my head and gather myself. "I'd better go talk to him, to make sure this won't become a bigger problem." I pause, glancing at both of them with a renewed blush tingling across my face. "Um, but it definitely wasn't a problem for me."

I hustle off after Landric before I can get any more embarrassed, with Iko's pleased laugh following me.

Landric has stalked all the way back to the stream. He's crouched down at the bank, peering into the water but giving the impression he's not actually seeing anything there.

At my approach, his gaze jerks up. He pushes to his feet and turns to face me, his expression tightening.

I stop a few paces away, my stomach balling into a hard lump. I just had one of the most amazing experiences of my life—why did this jerk have to ruin it?

"It wasn't even my idea," I blurt out. "Not that I'm saying it won't happen again. Not that it's any of your or anyone else's business."

The blotchy flush has crept back over Landric's face. His eyes flick down toward the ground and back to me. "I know it's not. I wasn't going to criticize."

I frown, crossing my arms over my chest. "You want to, though, don't you? You look like you're already thinking of all the new insults you could toss at me."

To my surprise, he flinches as if the accusation startles him. "Of course not. I wouldn't— I never said anything against you."

My eyebrows shoot up. "One of us has a very spotty memory, then."

Landric's hands twist the fabric of his tunic. "I know how it must have sounded. But whenever I heard anyone speak against you, I did my best to push them in another direction, to get their attention away from you so they'd leave you alone."

He did?

My mind careens back through all our brief encounters over the past several years. It's true that in most of them I remember someone else making the first jab or two, and him diverting them to some other topic. But the way he did it...

"You made it sound as if I wasn't worth bothering with."

Landric's head droops. "If I was too obviously defending you, everyone would have looked at me differently too."

My tone sharpens. "How horrible for you."

He meets my hard gaze with obvious effort, his dark

brown eyes simmering with emotions I don't understand. "I didn't want to make myself a target. I had things I was trying to accomplish… It was selfish, and all of that seems pointless now anyway. I'm sorry. I should have spoken up for you more, clearer. You didn't deserve any of it."

His voice has gone raw, every word searing with honest regret. My arms fall to my sides. I don't know what to do with his apology.

"What makes you so sure I didn't deserve it?" I find myself asking.

His expression turns incredulous. "So you overstepped when you were twelve. Twelve-year-olds aren't exactly the wisest human beings in the world. And you didn't get along with your aunt and uncle—well, I didn't find them to be the most agreeable people either. You took care of yourself without hurting anyone, even though the way we all acted must have hurt you. You even took the time to look after the memorial."

Landric hesitates and then offers me a cautious smile. "Thank you for that. I liked knowing that someone other than me cared."

His father's name was among the last few additions to the limestone walls that have since fallen. I hadn't realized he even noticed me going up there for the weekly cleanings.

I shift my weight. It feels as if the ground between us has tilted, and I'm no longer sure what to make of him.

He did speak up for me in front of everyone after we fled town. He's pulled his weight on this dangerous mission he volunteered for, from packing horse shit to charging into battle. The bandage on his arm shows how much he risked.

But how can I weigh that against all the times he listened to others disparage me and simply dismissed me as not worth even that much attention?

I drag in a breath. "All right. I'm not saying I'm okay

with what happened before. But we can move forward from that. There are bigger things to focus on."

Landric nods with a relieved air. His smile grows. "And you're the one who was brave enough to see how much we could do. Let's get back to our army and tell them it's time to really fight."

CHAPTER ELEVEN

Signy

J ostein squints through the darkness. "I think I see lantern light up there. That's probably them."

He nudges his horse from a walk to a trot, letting me nestle more closely against his chest. The feel of his body behind mine, his thighs braced against my hips, sets off even more warmth than it did before our little interlude with Iko.

We returned to the patch of forest where we left his captain and my neighbors in the wee hours of the night and found a message in some kind of military code. Apparently it meant that they'd moved to a spot east of the town. We don't know why that is or what exactly will be waiting for us there.

As we approach the woodlands up ahead, the first glow of sunlight hazes the sky. I make out a few tents between the trees and then a couple of soldiers in the burgundy Veldunian uniforms standing guard in the shadows.

Iko must recognize them, because he lifts his hand in a

wave. One of the soldiers returns the gesture and ducks farther into the forest.

By the time we've reached the trees and dismounted, Captain Amalia is striding over to join us. She looks us up and down with a bemused smile, her eyes bright.

"You really pulled it off," she says. "You're late, though. Was that you all the way over at the fort by Idam too?"

I shrug. "I thought we'd better make our point as well as possible."

"You did that." She glances over her shoulder toward the camp. "We relocated most of your neighbors to a few nearby settlements, but several dozen of them insisted on staying with us at least until we found out how your mission went. We've been gathering proper weapons for them... and speaking to other squadrons. I have people here eager to ride back to their captains and let them know when we're ready to mobilize."

My pulse hiccups at the thought of how much progress we've already made—how many people we've brought over to our side.

Jostein dips his head, his expression even more serious than usual. "We had help at the fort. A few of the locals went on to rally people in Vadan and Childeric. I told them to wait until they had our military backing them up before launching any new assaults, but I don't know how long they'll keep that in mind."

The captain nods. "We'll see about sending at least a squad to both towns to summon whoever's willing to join us —and continue spreading the word beyond there. We'll want to keep the main thrust of our force together. Picking at the empire bit by bit is fine for a start. It won't drive them out completely."

My gut twists at her implications, but the twinge of queasiness can't diminish my exhilaration. "Then the army's on board? You're going to help us push the Darium forces right out of Velduny?"

Captain Amalia's mouth tightens, but the gleam in her eyes only gets flintier. "They've had their way with our country for too long. If the four of you can manage to get the better of them, who am I to back down? We might never get a better chance."

Iko grins. "I knew I was glad when I got assigned to your squadron—and not just because I'd get to have a friend bossing me around." He elbows Jostein teasingly.

The captain gives him a wry look. "Come get something to eat and take a little rest. I can't imagine you've had much chance to do either with all the running around you've been doing. I need to reach out to my colleagues."

She must have prepped the squadron for our arrival, because as she steps away, a few other soldiers come forward to usher us over to a small campfire. Bowls of porridge are shoved into our hands. I gulp mine down so fast I scald my tongue.

One of the female soldiers directs me to a tent that it's clear someone else is also using, but they've already gotten up for the day. Now that I have the chance to relax, I'm too exhausted to do anything except crash on the sleeping bag and close my eyes.

I'm not sure how long I'm dead to the world, but raised voices and pounding feet jolt me out of sleep. With a lurch of my heart, I sit up and swipe at my bleary eyes.

Landric is pushing back the flap of my tent before I've made it that far. His voice comes out in a frantic hush. "A company of Darium soldiers is marching on another town south of here. The squadron and another that's just joined us are hurrying over to defend them."

He moves to the side so I can scramble out.

The camp has turned into a flurry of activity, soldiers and

some of my neighbors grabbing weapons and hustling away. Jostein is in their midst, calling out orders to arm themselves and picking who'll take the horses to reach the town first. He catches my gaze, and I dip my head to tell him I'm coming too.

Iko appears next to me, his blond hair tussled from his own interrupted sleep. "Let's get going before they can do even more damage."

Seeing Jostein ride ahead with a small group of soldiers sends an ache through my chest, but I can't pretend I'm battle-ready enough to be on the very front line. I strap my hunting knife in its sheath around my waist and rush to join the mass of us on foot.

We set off beyond the forest in the direction of the mountains. Captain Amalia stays with us, riding around the outskirts of our mismatched infantry and calling out orders and encouragement.

I notice a few people from Feldan sending curious glances my way. My aunt and uncle and Landric's mother are nowhere to be seen, but Bertha the butcher has stuck around, as has Norbert the cobbler—the latter to my surprise.

Do they all know that I've done more to conquer our enemies in the past few days than they have in their entire lives? What do they think of me now?

An echo of past humiliations prickles over my skin. I'm not sure I actually want to know.

Landric stays by my side, apparently committed to showing all of them that he's throwing his full support behind me. Iko marches nearby amid a group of his colleagues.

In the middle of the crowd, I can't see much other than the people marching ahead of me. I only know when the Darium forces have come into view from the angry cry that goes up from the soldiers at the front.

We pick up the pace instinctively. Captain Amalia pitches her voice to carry to all of us. "They're just reaching the town now. It looks like only a few dozen soldiers—we have them far outnumbered. Get in there and push them back however you can, but stick close to each other. Our strength is in working together."

It's a matter of minutes before shrieks and thumps reach my ears. I draw my hunting knife, my jaw clenching.

We pour into the outer streets of the town in a furious mass. The Darium soldiers who got there ahead of us bellow at us to back off, but no one listens.

They can't withstand the deluge.

The Veldunian soldiers at the front of the surge catch the boldest of the attackers, weapons clanging and bodies in skeleton uniforms crumpling. The pricks thought this place would be easy pickings, punishing innocent civilians for what their countryfolk have done elsewhere.

They're so very wrong.

Once the first several of their comrades have fallen, the Darium company must realize they're screwed. The bodies clad in black and white dash back the way they came, and we storm after them in determined pursuit.

One of them smashes a lantern and lights a ramshackle house near the edge of town on fire. A yelp goes up from inside.

I grab a bucket of water leftover from washing and douse the flames before they can do more than blacken the lower wall.

A soldier lunges at us from the side, but Iko is there, slashing the woman's neck open. We hurtle onward, out of the town, pressing the pillagers farther back.

Captain Amalia's voice rings through the ruckus, bringing us to a stop. She points toward the plain ahead of us.

The remaining Darium soldiers are fleeing toward a larger contingent in the skeletal uniforms. The front line is on horseback, with maybe a hundred foot-soldiers behind them.

The man riding a little ahead of the others sports a helm with a single red plume like a spurt of blood from its skull-like visage. I know that indicates he's someone higher up in the Darium army's ranks—tribune? Admiral?

He's also flying a small white flag indicating he means to parlay, not attack.

As the company marches toward us, I pick out some twenty figures in dark green uniforms off to the side. A gold crest gleams on the left side of their chests.

I frown. "Isn't that Duke Berengar's livery?"

Landric's stance goes rigid beside me. "Gods smite us, it sure looks like it."

Captain Amalia and a man on horseback who I think is also a captain as well ride forward to meet the approaching force. "That's close enough!" Amalia hollers.

We still have the advantage of numbers by a factor of about two, although nearly half of us are hardly soldiers. It must seem like enough of an imbalance that the Darium leader doesn't want to risk provoking us.

He holds up his hand for his people to draw to a halt and directs his horse forward on his own. He stops about ten paces from the company and the same from our captains. Then he swings down from his steed and steps in front of it as if sharing attention with even the animal would be unacceptable.

The delicate blue blossoms of sealace, just bloomed with the summer warmth, bob around his feet. It only grows in Velduny, but despite its looks, it's one of the hardiest plants out there.

I expect he'll find us an equally difficult challenge.

The military man doesn't lift his helm, letting its painted

skeletal face glower at us unchecked. His voice booms across the space between us.

"Veldunian insurgents, your disgraceful acts against the empire and your Darium benefactors will not be allowed to stand. This is your one chance to surrender before you—and the people you stand for—face the harsh punishment you deserve."

My skin itches uneasily. What does he think we deserve? All our towns and cities burned to the ground? Thousands slaughtered?

Captain Amalia has remained on her stallion. Her arm tenses at her side as if she'd like to grasp her sword and run this prick through right now.

"We don't intend to let you punish us," she retorts. "There'll be no surrendering unless it's on your side."

"I wouldn't be so hasty, traitor. The high commander who oversees this half of the continent is marching this way with an army far greater than anything you've been able to assemble. In a matter of days, the full might of the Darium empire will be prepared to crush your treachery."

Even though I know he's going out of his way to sound intimidating, my mouth dries up. Just how big an army is on its way? Will we be able to assemble enough people to fend them off?

How much will they destroy if we can't?

The Darium leader goes on without offering our side a chance to respond. "We'll give you ten minutes to decide. Surrender and hand over the woman named Signy who instigated this uprising, and High Commander Livius will treat the rest of you with more lenience."

All the blood seems to drain from my body, leaving me a cold husk.

He knows my name. He knows I started this.

Murmurs pass through the people gathered around us.

The soldiers remain stoically silent, but I catch fragments of anxious commentary from my neighbors.

"...comes down to her."

"An entire army!"

"...murder us all and..."

Landric reaches over to squeeze my hand, but I barely feel the contact. My mind has detached from my body, floating somewhere just behind it, like I can't bear to be part of myself.

Like the moment when I realized Inganne's gift wasn't coming, that no rush of magic was going to offset the throbbing of my foot where I'd offered my toes.

I went too far before. I pushed for more than I could handle and threw my life into shambles.

That's why she turned me away, isn't it? She knew I didn't only want to create beautiful things. I asked for a talent that people would envy and view with awe.

I wanted to show up my aunt and uncle for their grumbles and sighs, to make the rest of the town wish they'd pampered me in my grief rather than ignoring my struggles.

Is this rebellion really what's right for everyone, or have I only been acting out my own desire for vengeance? If I've overstepped again, it'll be far more than me paying for my arrogance.

The rest of the rebellion doesn't need me anyway. I could give myself up, buy my allies at least a little time, and they could decide when they're really ready without me pushing them on to the edge of ruin. Maybe they'd still be able to rally again and win our freedom.

But maybe they wouldn't. Maybe the spark of resistance would flicker out for good.

I swallow hard, my heart drumming against my ribs. Doubt constricts my lungs.

All I have to do is take one step forward and call out who I am...

The Darium leader turns on his heel. As he moves to his horse, he very deliberately brings his boot down on one of the sealace flowers.

He grinds it with a twist of his heel before he reaches for the saddle.

My spine stiffens. The murmurs fall away around me, and I know my companions have seen the gesture too.

No. We can't let the Darium empire grind us down even more. We're already shadows of ourselves, grasping at the scraps they've left us with.

Would I even have cared about the power of a gift if they hadn't stolen my parents from me, destroyed my childhood?

I've seen the light of hope come back into so many people's eyes in the past few days. *I* put it there—by demanding more, by doing more.

We need this. If we don't claim our victory now, if we let ourselves give up in despair, I don't know how we'll ever get that hope back.

I do take a step forward, but only to yell defiantly at the Darium company. "We won't be crushed. This is our country, and we're taking it back!"

A cheer louder than I was prepared for roars through the makeshift army around me. Townspeople and soldiers raise their weapons, ready for battle.

Captain Amalia smiles thinly and looks at the Darium side. "You've gotten your answer."

My fingers clench around the handle of my hunting knife, but the leader motions for his company to withdraw. "When you meet High Commander Livius, you'll regret that decision," he calls over his back.

I square my shoulders, gathering all my renewed resolve.

Not if I have anything to say about it.

CHAPTER TWELVE

Landric

I t's strange to realize that after all the hours I've spent in the company of the duke's son, I've never actually visited his family residence just an hour outside of Feldan. I always had to wait for Rupert to come to me.

I never had any delusions about him seeing me as a true equal, but as I rein in the horse Captain Amalia gave me leave to borrow, I feel just how expendable I've been to him on a deeper level than ever before.

How expendable we *all* are, possibly. The image of the guards in Duke Berengar's livery has haunted me since the confrontation with the Darium company yesterday.

The duke's son and heir might not see me as worthy of full consideration, but there's no one else from Feldan I can imagine him listening to at all. At least he'd decided I was one step up from a country hick.

If anyone's going to talk to him, it has to be me.

A guard in the same dark green jacket calls to me from the other side of the gate. "What's your business here?"

Not even a "sir" to soften the bluntness of the question, but then, I hardly cut a picture of refinement in my borrowed tunic and trousers that hang a little awkwardly on my body. I washed and tidied my hair as well as I could, but there's only so much you can do with nothing but streams and camp soap to work with.

"I need to speak to Master Rupert about an urgent matter," I say, attempting to make up for what I lack in appearance with lordly airs. "Tell him Landric from the town of Feldan is here—he knows me."

The guard grunts. "You'll need to wait at the gate."

He trots off to the residence, leaving a silent companion behind. I adjust my position in the saddle, not sure whether I should dismount or expect to ride on in.

It takes several minutes to get my answer, with the thud of two sets of footsteps across the lane on the other side. I've swung out of the saddle before the guard can even open the gate, knowing Rupert will respond better if we're on level footing rather than me looking down at him.

He strides out to meet me, his broad chest even more puffed up than usual but his eyes warily narrow. "Landric! I wasn't expecting to see you."

There are a lot of ways I could interpret that sentence. I decide it doesn't really matter exactly what he's implying.

I bob my head deferentially, as he'll appreciate. "I apologize for the intrusion. I needed to speak with you—I'm sure you heard what happened to Feldan."

Rupert grimaces. "A bad business, that, but not unexpected after an act of revolt. I trust your mother was able to evacuate safely?"

The fact that he bothers to ask gives me a tiny spark of hope. "Yes, thank the gods." My fingers sketch down my front automatically in the gesture of the divinities. She's joined the refugees who were taken in by one of the nearby towns. "But the threat isn't over yet. We've been warned that a large Darium force is marching on Velduny."

"That's not surprising either, with the continued attacks on Darium posts. Some kind of order needs to be restored."

My stomach twists. I remember all too well the way he spoke when we watched the celebration in the town square. "I heard that some of your family's guards rode with the Darium soldiers." Better not to admit outright that I was there to witness them myself.

Rupert doesn't even hesitate to nod. "My father knows where he owes his loyalty. We were glad to supply whatever support they'd find useful."

I wet my lips, choosing my next words carefully. "Seeing how events have played out so far, I can't help wondering if there might be a real chance of regaining Velduny's freedom… if enough of us banded together. We could be loyal only to—"

The duke's son cuts me off with a scoffing sound. "Challenge the entire Darium army? You sound as mad as that Signy must be. Of course it'd all start with the waif of refuse."

A chill trickles through my veins at his words. When the Darium tribune asked for her, I hadn't wanted to think—but Rupert and his friends were the only people outside of Feldan who knew that Signy instigated the revolt. The only people who could have mentioned it to our enemies.

"You told them about her," I say evenly, not even a question.

"The blame should be dealt out fairly." Rupert chuckles. "I can't imagine why those upstarts haven't given her up already. What about her is worth preserving?"

My teeth set on edge, but I'm as much frustrated with myself as with him. Stung by the memories of all the times I let statements like that stand or even tacitly agreed with them.

I can't shout at him the way I'd like to right now. Jabbing at his ego might make him even more eager to see Signy destroyed.

But I won't keep quiet either.

"Perhaps that should be a sign that there's more to her than you've recognized." I turn back to my horse. It's clear I'm not going to make any progress with Rupert, and anything more I say could incite him to have me detained. "I hope you evaluate your loyalties with all due care."

Rupert's eyes narrow again. "Landric, what are you saying?"

"Just a bit of common wisdom." I haul myself back onto the horse and nudge it to a canter without another word, leaving the duke's son staring after me. "I should get back to helping my neighbors recuperate."

Just not in the way I hope he thinks. Great God help me, let me not have soured the situation even further.

I have a couple of hours' journey to our current camp to reflect on the conversation and what I'm going to say when I return. I didn't speak to anyone except for Captain Amalia before I left, but I suspect Signy will have noticed my absence by now.

I wish I was bringing better news. I wish I'd accomplished anything at all with my little quest.

By the time the procession of soldiers, civilians, and pack-laden horses comes into view up ahead, I've considered all the possibilities and settled on the bald truth as my best option. Get it over with, move on.

The three captains now leading our uprising have us moving to the east, so we'll be ready to stand against the Darium army before they can rampage through any major settlements. New allies have been joining us by the hour, drifting in from towns that have caught word of our efforts, but still Signy takes note of my arrival before I've quite reached the edge of the march. Her leanly athletic figure comes into view veering off in my direction, the two soldiers who've become her biggest advocates close at her heels.

At the sight of her companions, the image flickers through my mind of the two men with their arms around her, their mouths claiming her lips and neck. Jealousy flares up inside me, burning my cheeks and constricting my throat.

She really didn't understand why it rattled me, seeing that. I'm so far from a potential suitor to her that it never even occurred to her I might want to court her.

Who do I have to blame for that other than myself? From nearly the first moment they met her, Jostein and Iko have stood by her, spoken up for her.

Why wouldn't she want them?

Pushing down the churn of my emotions, I dismount when I've come abreast with her. My horse will need some time to cool down at a walk and then one of the soldiers like Jostein will no doubt claim the animal.

"Where did you go?" Signy demands before I can so much as open my mouth.

Her sharp green eyes pin me in place. Jostein and Iko are watching me too, but I barely feel their gazes compared to hers.

I push my mouth into my best wry smile. "I went to the duke's estate. I wanted to see—"

Signy's stance tenses. "You went to the *dukeling*? After everything that's happened, you're still trying to impress—"

"No!" I break in. "I don't give a shit what Rupert thinks of me now. I only thought—I could at least find out exactly where they stand—if there was any hope of persuading them to oppose Dariu—"

Iko, who doesn't even know the duke or his son, snorts,

and a shamed heat floods my body. The idea didn't seem so absurd when I first thought of it.

Signy folds her tan arms over her chest. "They already offered their guards up to the Darium army. It's obvious which side they prefer to be on. How could you still think you could trust them?"

I swallow thickly. "I didn't, not really. I just wanted to try. To do *something*."

Jostein studies me with his usual authoritative calm. Whatever he thinks of my attempt, he doesn't reveal any disdain in his voice. "What did they say?"

"They're totally committed to supporting the empire," I admit. "And... Rupert's the one who pointed the finger at Signy."

Her eyes flash. "Of course he was. You only just figured that out?"

My words stall in my throat. It was the obvious answer. Maybe there is something wrong with my own loyalties that I didn't fully believe it, didn't want to believe it, until I heard it from him directly.

But even when his opinion mattered to me the most, even when it seemed as if all my dreams of getting out of Feldan depended on his good will, I never felt half as desperate as I do right now.

I meet Signy's piercing gaze, letting it hollow me out. I wanted to do something to help our cause, but all I've done is make her question *my* loyalty. My fucking common sense.

And I don't know if I can tolerate a world in which this woman looks at me with suspicion any longer.

How did I never realize just how spectacular she is before? These two men saw it so quickly.

She's single-handedly set a revolution in motion, rallied hundreds to the cause, seen the ways to cut through the empire's bullshit.

All the dreams I once had are nothing but shadows compared to the future she's aimed us toward.

I don't really care where in the world I end up or what I'm doing there, as long as I'm at her side seeing what she'll do next.

So everything I do from here forward, it has to be proving myself to her. Earning her trust, her friendship... I don't know if I can dare to hope for more than that.

It doesn't matter. I'll take as much or as little as I can get as long as I can be here with her.

No resolution has ever felt so right. The decision steadies me.

"I'm sorry," I say. "Old habits die hard, but this one couldn't be more deceased. We don't need the help of the nobles anyway, not when we've got you pointing the way. What's the best thing I can do for our revolution right now?"

CHAPTER THIRTEEN

Signy

"Block, feint, jab," Jostein calls out, stepping forward with a swing of his sword.

I jerk the short sword I was given this morning through the motions we've been practicing. Steel clangs against steel, the impact reverberating through my arms.

I manage not to stumble backward like I did the first few times we practiced this sequence, but my jab isn't quite fast enough to even nick Jostein's tunic before he's smacking my blade aside.

As I grimace in frustration, he lowers his sword and squeezes my shoulder. "You're doing well. Most of us had years of training and practice battles before we saw real enemy action." He glances across the field around us. "I'm sure we never expected to find ourselves as the teachers this early in our careers."

All across the lightly hilly terrain around us, other soldiers are directing the civilians who've joined our ranks through similar exercises. The periodic influxes of new squadrons have brought some extra weapons with them, and some people are still using kitchen and hunting knives, makeshift spears, or whatever else we could scrounge up to arm them.

My gaze drifts farther to the peaks looming in the distance. It's a strange sensation, looking over and finding the mountains at my flank rather than up ahead.

We've come a long way from Feldan. But if we want to stop the Darium army from terrorizing any towns or villages of innocent Veldunians in their rampage to end our rebellion, we have to be on the front lines. We're at the eastern edge of the country here, only twenty miles shy of the border with Icar.

I hope the army the emperor is sending won't take their anger out on the innocent civilians of the other countries they have to travel through. Although the thought sends a tingle of exhilaration through my veins—what if every country Dariu has subjugated found the courage to rise up against them?

What if the whole continent could be free again?

The touch of Iko's hand on my side brings me back to the present with a different sort of tingle. The soldier leans close, adjusting my stance and the angle of my sword, his body warming my back.

"If you keep the blade tilted to the side, you protect more of you from attack," he says in a low voice that makes me think of all the thrilling things we could be doing other than engaging in mock battles. "And always keep one foot at least a little ahead of the other for ease of dodging."

His hand drops to my hip to nudge one leg forward, and heat flares between my thighs. His breath tickles over my neck.

I can't help thinking of the press of his lips against the

sensitive skin there a few nights ago. Of being enveloped by both of these men.

But this isn't the time or place to be indulging in those sorts of thrills.

As Iko eases back, Jostein looks at him with a slight arch of his eyebrows. "If you're done groping her…"

Iko laughs. "I don't think Signy minds getting some hands-on instruction."

My cheeks flush, and the look Jostein gives me, a smolder lighting in his bright blue eyes, makes me reconsider the whole "we probably shouldn't make out on the training field" principle I've been following.

"I would also like to make sure I don't *die* when we're facing an entire Darium army," I say, pleased that my voice only comes out a tiny bit breathless. "So let's continue the regular instruction."

Jostein raises his sword, and a yelp rings out from across the field.

My head jerks around with a lurch of my pulse, but all I see is one of the new trainees rubbing his eyes frantically, an orange flower bobbing in a patch of weed near his feet.

"You need to flush your eyes with water to clear out the pollen," I holler over to him. I had an unfortunate encounter with lissweld in bloom back when I was a kid, and rubbing only made the stinging worse. It took a few hours before I could see properly again.

As the man hurriedly gropes for a canteen, Captain Amalia rides by, surveying the situation with a frown. With the amplification charm she's been using since our numbers started to grow, she pitches her voice over the entire field. "Remember to watch out for the lissweld flowers! We have enough enemies already without fighting pollen too."

Chuckles pass through our crowd at her wry tone, and everyone takes a careful look at the ground around us. We didn't have a whole lot of choice in where we stationed our line of resistance.

"At least we avoided that huge patch of the stuff back there," I say, motioning behind us to where we passed a stretch of dense blooms that must have gone on for a quarter of a mile. I waggle my blade. "Where were we?"

Jostein swipes his sleeve across his forehead, sweat beading under the midday sun. "Let's go back to that side-step and stab combo you were making progress with before. Every soldier needs to learn to lean into their strengths. You're going to get farther with speed and nimbleness than brute strength."

We run through the motions with Iko observing and offering a little commentary. By the fourth attempt, I manage to tap my sword against Jostein's side.

A grin springs to my face. "You'd better not have let me land that blow."

Jostein shakes his head. "What would you learn from that? You're getting faster—and better at spotting the openings."

He pauses to brush back a strand of hair that's blown across my face, his fingers grazing my cheek. A renewed warmth blooms across my skin.

Maybe I should be training with his colleagues rather than him and Iko. These stunning men are way too distracting.

But I don't trust anyone else here even half as much as I do them.

At that thought, my gaze moves across the field instinctively. I haven't consciously registered who I'm looking for until my eyes snag on Landric's well-built form in the midst of his own training.

His coppery hair has darkened with sweat, but he's clearly putting his all into the brief sparring match with the soldier who's been helping him. There's something pretty stunning about his face too when it's set in that mask of determination.

I yank my attention back to the men I'm standing with. The apologies and promises Landric has made to me, the passion that reverberated through his voice, echo through my memory. They're a distraction too.

"How long have the two of you been serving rather than training?" I ask as I raise my sword to resume our practice. Neither Jostein nor Iko look like they're out of their twenties.

Iko lifts his chin toward Jostein. "Jos graduated from the military school at our duchy's main temple of Sabrelle a year before I did—benefits of managing to be born a year earlier. It's been six years of active service for him, five for me."

Curiosity tickles at me. "Is that where you two met?" They haven't mentioned any shared history outside of their military experiences.

Jostein nods and twitches his sword toward his friend. "This one was a trouble-maker from the start despite all that supposed Esterean wisdom. I got assigned to 'guide him onto a smoother path.'"

"Which only half worked," Iko puts in with a grin. "I'm partly incorrigible."

There's obvious fondness in the squad leader's tone. "But after four years of schooling together, he grew on me."

The warmth of their dynamic sends an odd pang through me. I have no idea what it's like to have a friendship like that —one so close and loyal they didn't even let their shared interest in the same woman divide them.

But maybe, by living alongside them for the past week, I'm starting to get a taste of it. The affection in Jostein's gaze when it returns to me might be more heated, but I know it also matters to him to prepare me for the upcoming battles as well as possible.

Neither of them have been shy about showing I mean much more to them than a means of scratching an itch.

Jostein resumes his sparring stance, but before we can attempt another exercise, hoofbeats thunder over the nearest low hill. One of the sentries our commanders sent ahead gallops toward us with an urgent shout. "Captains!"

Without needing to say a word, Jostein, Iko, and I exchange a worried glance and hustle over to find out what's happened.

The five captains now with us and a major who arrived with more troops yesterday gather to meet the sentry. As the three of us push closer, many other soldiers and civilians draw nearer. Tension hums through the air.

The sentry doesn't even bother to dismount. As soon as he reaches the leaders of our ragtag band, he reins in his horse and starts speaking at an urgent clip. "The Darium army is almost here! They're approaching the border now, coming through Icar."

A chill washes over me. If they're almost at the border, they could be on us by tomorrow.

The major frowns. "How large a force have they sent?"

The sentry draws in a breath, a tremor passing through his slim frame. "There had to be thousands of them. Three, maybe four?"

My gaze darts across the mass of figures around us. We've assembled a force several hundred strong, but we'll still be overwhelmed... and all of the Darium soldiers will have had far more than a few days' worth of training. They'll all have proper weapons and armor.

Major Arlo glances at the captains. Technically he has the most military authority among us, but he hasn't been lording his higher title over the other officers, recognizing that most of them have been directly involved in the rebellion for longer than he has. "If we're going to win this, it won't be through might. We'll need Estera and Kosmel watching over us as much as Sabrelle."

As if any of the godlen of wisdom, trickery, or war are watching out for us now. What we really need is to keep our own wits about us.

Captain Amalia lifts her head. "We have a few advantages we can make use of. Emperor Vitus has sent soldiers from abroad—few if any of them will be familiar with Velduny's terrain. We know our country as they can't."

Murmurs of agreement pass through the watching crowd, but her words don't reassure me that much. We've always known our country better than the Darium forces, but it hasn't allowed us to fend them off in the past.

We have to use that knowledge in the right way. How are the hills around us or the distant mountains going to help us defeat an entire army?

"We should warn the nearest towns and villages," one of the other captains is saying. "Most of them didn't want to evacuate before, but if they know the threat is so close by…"

Another peers at the landscape around us. "Is there any ideal location between here and the border where we could stage an ambush?"

The wind picks up, tossing bits of dried grass and grit into the air. A woman on the other side of the gathering swipes at her eyes to clear them, and inspiration lights in my head like a flame in a lantern.

"I have an idea," I blurt out.

The major and the five captains all turn to look at me. I expect one of them to tell me off for interrupting, but they all study me with interest… possibly even hope. Waiting for me to say more.

Pride expands through my chest alongside a burst of nerves.

I've proven myself—I spearheaded this rebellion. They're willing to listen to me.

I set us on this course, and I'd better not lead us astray.

Inhaling deeply, I sort through my thoughts, making sure I'm confident in them before I speak. Maybe the gods are watching over us right now; maybe Inganne sparked the idea in my head, letting me picture the scene I could create.

Jostein's hand rests on my back, a tacit support. Iko shoots me an encouraging smile. And farther around the crowd, I catch Landric's gaze on me.

I'm not in this alone, not anymore.

"We have several people who've joined us who have gifts for building, don't we?" I ask to confirm. The captains have been compiling a list of all the magic every new arrival can offer as they appear. "Who can move objects with their will?"

It's a common gift to appeal to Creaden for, since that godlen presides over construction as well as leadership. Much easier to build walls and roofs if you can stand back and direct the materials with your mind.

Captain Amalia nods. "Not enough that they could enhance our weapons a significant amount."

The corner of my mouth quirks upward. "Not our traditional weapons. It'll be risky, but… I think we can arrange for our countryside to do a lot of the fighting for us."

CHAPTER FOURTEEN

Signy

"Gods save us," Bertha mutters where she's crouched on the hilltop next to me. "Here they come."

The mass of figures in their white-on-black uniforms has appeared on the horizon. They march forward across the landscape like a rigid flood—perfectly regimented, perfectly steady, but with a momentum that feels inevitable.

Unstoppable.

My lungs constrict. I have to force myself to drag in a deep breath of the warm air to try to loosen the tension.

The Darium army isn't unstoppable. We've cut down soldiers like these more than once in the recent past.

But never anywhere near so many. Never when they were utterly bent on our destruction.

At my other side, Landric shifts his position with an air of restlessness he's trying to suppress. "Don't move until they've almost reached the crossroads. We've got a little time left."

When they come up on the crossroads, they'll have the

option of veering north and laying waste to the first village on this side of the border. It's a quaint place without even a temple to call its own, only a cluster of houses and a couple of common buildings surrounded by farms.

When we warned them, a few of the inhabitants opted to join our cause. A few fled to camp out in the forest farther north. Others refused to leave their homes at all.

They'll all lose those homes if the army heads that way. We've seen how thorough Dariu likes to be in dealing out revenge.

There won't be a single building left standing.

So we have to make sure they come this way.

I scan the fields on either side of the road for any splotches of orange we missed. With a waft of relief, I find none.

Most of our "army" spent the better part of the past day ever-so-carefully plucking any lissweld blooms we could find and adding them to the thicker field that's currently at our backs. We didn't want the Darium soldiers stumbling on a patch early and realizing the danger the flowers pose.

It isn't just our familiarity with our country that works to our advantage. The Darium forces are ignorant in all sorts of ways.

They don't know that our numbers have doubled since the last time one of their representatives confronted our resistance. They don't know how organized we've become under the guidance of our own military leaders.

Let them think we're merely a scruffy band of resentful townspeople who can barely handle a knife, let alone a sword. They're marching on us assuming there's no way we can stand against them.

Their arrogance is our greatest advantage of all.

A large man on a massive stallion rides in the center of the army, several scarlet plumes jutting from his helm. That must be High Commander Livius, the one we were warned about.

The man who's given the ultimate orders to every Darium soldier in this half of the continent. The man who's overseen our subjugation.

As Landric watches the army approach, he twists his fingers into the grass by his knees. He's pulled a brown cap over his distinctive reddish hair so it doesn't catch the sunlight, but a few ruddy tufts poke out along the nape of his neck.

I shouldn't notice things like that. I shouldn't want to talk to him—but I don't really know what to make of him these days.

He smiled when I explained my plan and told me it was brilliant. He volunteered to be on the front lines of this mission before we even asked who'd take that risk.

How much is he the same man he used to be, after everything we've been through?

"I suspect this isn't the kind of exploring the world you were thinking of when you imagined your future," I murmur to him.

His mouth slants into a crooked grin that takes his face from handsome to breathtaking. "No, not quite. It's certainly more exciting. And it'll matter leagues more than anything I ever pictured myself doing."

Bertha snorts. "*Exciting.*"

Landric lifts his shoulders in a slight shrug. "I'm not saying I wouldn't skip the hand-to-hand combat parts if I could. But... my whole life, I just wanted the chance to roam around the countryside freely. Now we could be part of giving everyone in Velduny their freedom. Nothing else seems all that important."

The tightness in my chest creeps up to my throat. "Yeah."

Those words resonate with me more than I'd have

expected. What do statues and paintings matter when I'm helping create a more beautiful future for all of us who've lived under the Darium empire's thumb?

What we're going to do here today will be a kind of masterpiece, and I'm the one who sculpted it.

The Darium army has continued their relentless advance. Iko's voice carries from behind us. "It's almost time. Is everyone ready?"

Voices lift in answer all across the hillside. Several dozen of us have gathered for this first part of the plan.

We need to present a big enough force that the Darium soldiers will be sure we're part of the main resistance without putting too many of our people in the most extreme danger.

Captain Amalia, the only higher officer who joined us, treads across the grass behind me. "Be fast on your feet, everybody. Just harass them—don't get any closer than you need to. Just enough for them to follow. *Now.*"

At her command, we spring to our feet and hurtle down the hill toward the road. Up ahead, the Darium army is little more than ten paces shy of the crossroads.

A shout goes up the moment we race into view, but there's nothing panicked about the sound. They won't see our small group as a significant threat.

Their mistake. I bet we can take down a few of them even now.

The Veldunian soldiers among us in their plain clothes and a few of the ordinary civilians with hunting practice brandish their bows of all sorts. As they send a volley of arrows shrieking through the air toward the enemy, the rest of us holler insults at the top of our lungs. I pull back the slingshot Iko constructed for me and fling one sharp stone and then another with all the force I can bring to bear.

The Darium soldiers on the front line jerk up their shields—black painted with interlaced bones to match their uniforms. Most of the arrows and other projectiles glance off the steel surfaces of those and their helms, but I see one plunge into a man's shoulder, another catching a woman in the throat. A few figures stagger amid their comrades.

I reach for another rock, but High Commander Livius jerks a rigid arm forward. His booming voice carries across the terrain, amplified by magic. "Crush these pathetic miscreants!"

The Darium army surges toward us at his command. Captain Amalia yells the order for us to retreat.

We could have fled faster on horseback, but presenting ourselves as an armed cavalry rather than common rabble would make the Darium force more cautious. So we dash away on foot, our boots thumping along the road between the low hills.

It's half a mile. Half a mile past the field of lissweld to where the rest of our allies are waiting.

Half a mile before we're out of pollen range and our gifted companions can cast out their magic.

We aren't the only ones with bows. As the pounding of tramping feet reverberates from behind us, arrows plunge into our midst. There's a cry and a thud of a falling body behind me. A bit of fletching grazes my ear as a shaft twangs by.

I swallow a yelp and push myself faster. "Come on, everyone!" I call out, but my voice sounds hoarse.

More arrows whir through the air. More gasps of pain and ominous thumps carry from around me.

I glance over just as one pointed shaft rams into Bertha's back. A noise of protest breaks from my throat as she crumples.

"Signy!" Landric grabs my elbow, yanking me to the side. An arrow that might have speared me through my own back slices across my bicep instead.

Pain sears all through my arm with a spurt of blood. I can't do anything but keep running.

Orange blooms flare at the edge of my vision. We're passing the field. We're leading the Darium soldiers straight toward it.

I throw myself forward, my companions charging onward as if we're one being. There isn't time to look around and see how many we've lost.

We knew this was a dangerous gambit, but it wasn't half as dangerous as trying to face the army on even ground.

"Anyone injured, continue back behind our front lines," the captain is hollering.

Iko appears beside me, his eyes widening as he takes in my wound. He slings his arm around my back and urges me the last short distance to where our larger force is waiting.

The rest of the rebels don't charge to meet the Darium soldiers, not yet. The moment our contingent acting as bait races past the field, a smattering of figures raise their hands.

Their magic propels the very air.

A wind whips up over the field and flings the lissweld's pollen away from us, toward the advancing soldiers. A flurry of pale yellow whirls across the landscape like a sudden blizzard.

The tiny grains patter against shields and helms—and slip through the gaps in the visors.

All at once, the first barrage of Darium soldiers lurch and stumble. One and another claw at their helms. Watching, I'm barely aware of the army medic who's stopped by my side to murmur a little healing magic over my arm. A smile curves my lips.

I can just imagine the agony they're feeling, the stinging sensation digging into their eyeballs, the world around them turned into a vague blur as their vision fogs with irritation and tears.

Take that, you vicious pricks.

More wind gusts over the army, sending the searing pollen all through their ranks. Their strict formation is shattering into chaos.

High Commander Livius wheels on his horse, hollering orders I can't make out. Then our major flings his hand forward.

Several hundred soldiers and armed civilians dash forward to attack our disabled opponents. Blades plunge into guts and slice through throats. Clubs bash in helms and fracture bones.

Blood splatters scarlet across the grass next to the sea of orange flowers.

I step forward, reaching for the short sword at my hip, but the medic catches my arm. "The injured stay back. Captain's orders."

So I simply watch the carnage with grim satisfaction. The bodies of our colleagues, struck down on our mad dash here, have been lost amid the swarm of soldiers. But we're taking down so many more of them than they stole from us.

The high commander must realize they're currently outmatched. More shouts ring out, and the soldiers at the back of the march start retreating, just a few at first and then in a more orderly mass, surging away from the scene of destruction even faster than they swept down on us. The plumed helmet bobs away from us.

As my fellow rebels continue to carve through the nearest enemies, a cheer of victory goes up. We've sent them running. We've taken down hundreds of our foes.

A swell of triumph fills my chest, but it's dampened by the sight of all those dark uniforms pulling away from us.

There are still thousands more of them, and now they know we're a force to be reckoned with. We've won this battle, but we haven't won the war.

We leave the Darium corpses where they fell, murmuring a prayer for our fallen comrades among them, and draw back to the shelter of the nearest forestland. While we roast deer and wild boar our allies have hunted down, our sentries report that the Darium army has withdrawn all the way to the border to regroup.

That gives us at least a day's buffer before they can strike at us again. A day to come up with another plan that'll let us come out ahead—and most of us alive.

The voices and laughter that resonate around the campfires have a celebratory vibe, but I keep seeing Bertha slumping with the arrow in her back. Keep searching the faces around me to try to determine exactly how many people we lost today.

How many people died carrying out my plan.

I'm not the only one with loss on my mind. My eyes catch Jostein's through the crowd for the first time since the attack, and he barrels past the figures around us with a frantic light in his bright blue eyes.

The squad leader comes to a halt in front of me, his gaze darting over my face, his bronze-brown skin looking grayed. "You're all right? I heard you were injured—I've been looking for you."

The intensity of his concern makes my pulse stutter. I motion vaguely toward the torn, bloody fabric of my sleeve, the pink line where the medic healed the broken flesh beneath. "Just a minor wound. They patched me up."

Jostein's mouth twists. "It came so close."

He touches my arm, his expression so fraught it wrenches at me. There's blood speckled across his tunic too, and a deepening purple bruise on his cheek that wasn't there before.

We all toed a perilous line today. We're all lucky not to be one of the few wrenched over the edge.

Gods help me, what would I have done if the Darium soldiers had murdered this man in front of me?

The anguish that rushes through me at that thought reflects back at me from Jostein's face. His hand rises to touch my cheek. Heat tingles across my skin, both from his touch and the mix of fear and longing in his gaze.

"I've just found you," he says in a strained voice. "There's so much we haven't had time for... I can't lose you."

I know he's talking about more than finding me just now in the crowd. My body sways toward him of its own accord, my hand coming to rest on his chest. "I'm right here. I'm not going anywhere."

A raw sound thrums from his throat, and then he pulls me into a kiss.

CHAPTER FIFTEEN

Signy

I've kissed Jostein before, but it was nothing like this. His fingers tangle in my hair; his mouth captures mine with an urgent passion as if he needs me to survive.

The heady rush of the embrace floods my body. I kiss him back with all I have, giving myself over to the moment, to the thump of my pulse and the sparks racing through my nerves, confirming how alive we both are.

I grip the front of his tunic, caught up in the need to pull him even closer. My desire flares all the way down to the apex of my thighs.

We just did something crazy and incredible, and it won't be the last time. There's no telling what might become of either of us when we next face the Darium army.

I don't want to think about that. I want to revel in the fact that we're still here right now—that I matter to this daring, valiant man.

When Jostein draws back just enough for our mouths to

part, his breath tingling over my lips, I murmur, "Have you got a tent?"

A partly suppressed groan escapes him, and then he's ushering me with him, his arm at my back and his hand twined with mine. His musky scent and the heat of his body drown out all but the vaguest impressions of the comrades we pass on our weaving path between the trees.

Our soldiers have been pitching tents all around the campsite. Jostein leads me to one at the farthest edge— because of course he'd want to be the first line of defense.

I can't be anything but glad for it now, because it means we're well beyond watching eyes when he pushes back the flap and we duck inside.

The moment we're kneeling together within the low, sloping walls, Jostein's mouth descends on mine.

He's been careful with me in the past, sometimes almost tentative, but it must have been because he didn't want to overstep his welcome. There's nothing but confidence in the way he handles me now, angling our heads to deepen the kiss, guiding my knee over his legs so I'm straddling him.

He's a man who knows what he wants. A man who's meant to be leading, even if his superiors haven't yet recognized just how much authority he can wield.

I sit back on his thighs, splaying my hands against his well-muscled chest, and gaze at him with a spark of mischief tickling through my veins. "It seems I'm at your disposal, squad leader. How would you command me?"

Only faint lantern light filters through the canvas walls of the tent, but it's enough to reveal the answering glint in Jostein's eyes. His posture pulls a little straighter.

As he rests his hands on my hips, his voice comes out low but resonant. "Let's have that shirt off so I can appreciate even more of you, rebel maiden."

With a soft laugh, I reach to peel off both my blood-stained tunic and the thin undershirt beneath. The cool evening air washes over my bared skin.

Jostein's gaze drinks me in through the dimness. A brief doubt flickers through my thoughts—all those years of scrounging for food have left my ribs visible through my flesh, and I've hardly got the fullest breasts around—but when he brings his mouth back to mine, I feel nothing but hunger.

He kisses me with all the intensity he showed before. One hand rises to skim the slight curve of my breast and then cup it completely. His palm swivels against my nipple with a jolt of pleasure, and I gasp against his mouth.

Jostein hums in approval and eases away just far enough to yank off his own shirt. He pulls me close against him, skin to skin, one hand massaging my other breast while he reclaims my mouth.

The arm at my back slides down almost to my ass and tugs me closer. My sex settles against the bulge straining against Jostein's pants.

I rock against it, propelled by my growing need, and he gives a strangled growl. His lips trail from my mouth to nip the edge of my jaw.

"Lean back," he says in his commanding voice.

I'm all too happy to comply. As I tip against his supporting arm, he ducks his head to chart a scorching path along the side of my neck and down my chest.

When his mouth closes over the peak of my breast, I clutch his shoulder with a whimper. He rolls the nub beneath his tongue and tugs it between his lips, setting off pulse after pulse of bliss.

As he shifts to the side to be thorough in his attentions, my hand rises to grip his close-cropped hair. At the stroke of my fingertips over his scalp, Jostein makes an encouraging sound that reverberates from his throat to delightful effect.

He sucks my nipple deeper into his mouth with a sweep of his tongue, massaging my ass at the same time. When I grind against his erection, a breath shudders out of him.

He pulls my face back toward him, his gaze seeking out mine, his eyes intent despite the darkening of lust. "I want to make you feel every pleasure imaginable tonight, but I'm not looking just to get off. The past few days... I can't imagine my life feeling whole unless you stay in it, Signy."

Despite the ache of desire that's gripping me, my throat constricts. How can any of us know what the future will hold, what he'll want after we see this rebellion through?

But we don't even know if we *will* see it through. And there's nothing I'd like to believe more than that I could stay in this man's life, whatever place I could find there. It isn't as if I have a home to go back to.

"If I have anything to say about it, you won't need to imagine," I murmur.

A brilliant smile crosses Jostein's face. He cups my face between his calloused hands and kisses me so hard I can barely remember anything exists except him.

I press into him again, the needy ache between my thighs getting hotter by the second. With a rough chuckle, Jostein tilts us over to lie on our sides on the spread sleeping mats. He ducks his head to lap the peak of my breast back into his mouth while delving one hand beneath the waist of my trousers.

At the first brush of his fingers over my clit, I have to bite back a moan. Jostein caresses me through my dampened drawers and then slides his hand right beneath the thinner fabric. I rock with his explorations, my hold on him tightening when he dips a finger right inside me.

Then, with a warble of fabric, the tent flap pulls back.

I freeze, and Jostein's head jerks up.

Iko leans inside, his eyes gleaming and his striking face holding one of his sly grins. "I thought I noticed you two sneaking off over here. What happened to sharing, Jos?"

Jostein's eyes start to narrow into a glower, but at the same moment, his friend's words and the images they stir up set off a fresh pulse of desire through my body. To be touched like this by both of these men, the way they encompassed me in their kisses and caresses the other night...

Arousal pools in my sex with an eager quiver, and Jostein hesitates. He pumps his testing finger in and out of me while his friend watches, and his smile returns.

"What are you waiting for, then?" he asks Iko with a hint of a growl. "Get in here and let's see that our woman is properly celebrated."

Iko shows no sign of offense at being ordered around. He enters the tent and sprawls out at my back, immediately teasing one hand over my bare belly while he sweeps aside my hair with the other to kiss my neck.

Oh, gods. All I can do is tremble and sway between the two men as Jostein brings his mouth back to mine and Iko starts to fondle my breasts. The bigger man adds a second finger inside me, and I whimper into his mouth.

With a guttural sound, Jostein yanks down my trousers and drawers together. "I need to feel you around me."

Having no interest in arguing, I fumble with the fastening on his pants. He guides one of my legs all the way up to his waist and enters me with one swift thrust.

"Fuck," I mumble, the sensation of being so perfectly filled rippling through my entire body. I'm so wet there's barely any friction at all as he pumps in and out of me, only the sweet burn of being stretched in just the right way.

Iko muffles a groan against my hair, pressing against me from behind as if to urge me on. As I buck with Jostein's thrusts, he delves his hand between us.

When Iko's fingers glide over my clit, I have to slam my mouth against Jostein's to smother my moan. Iko circles his fingers around that most sensitive spot and nips my shoulder, Jostein plunges even deeper, and I can feel any shred of control I had left spiraling away from me.

I careen over the edge in a burst of pleasure that tingles all the way to my toes. My body shudders, lost in the flood.

My sex clamps around Jostein, and words spill out of him in a nearly incoherent muttering. "So good. Fucking incredible. Signy. Gods."

After a couple more thrusts, I know he's followed me. His head bows toward mine, and he holds me against him as if we could stay this way forever.

Iko nuzzles the back of my neck and peppers gentle kisses across my shoulder blades. He trails his hand up and down my abdomen as I come down from the orgasmic high.

"It's an honor to witness you coming apart, Spitfire," he murmurs.

Jostein presses his lips to mine once more and peers over me at his friend. He palms my breast with a flick of his thumb over the nipple, bringing it back to full stiffness. "You could do better than witness it. I'd imagine she could be even more satisfied."

A giddy quiver shoots through me at his suggestion.

Iko lets out a light, breathless laugh and rolls me toward him. As I find myself straddling him, he grins up at me. "What do you think, Signy? Ready for another round?"

A flush spreads over my skin with a renewed throb of longing.

How is this my life? How have I ended up with two men who want me like this?

I can't see any point in denying that I want him too.

I set my hand against the erection straining against his trousers, getting a deeper thrill out of the ecstatic expression that crosses his face. "I think you've got too many clothes on."

With another laugh, he wrenches at his trousers. "A problem we can easily solve."

As Iko kicks off his pants, Jostein sits up next to us. He teases his fingers down my spine and along my inner thigh, apparently as intent on adding to my enjoyment as his friend was during our coupling.

Iko eases me down onto him slowly, inch by inch, dragging out the pleasure of the penetration. An impatient noise works from my throat, and he chuckles.

Propping himself up on one elbow, he grasps my hair and tugs me to him for our first real kiss tonight. As our mouths meld together, he rolls his hips and consumes my gasp of pleasure.

With a smile now purely wicked, Iko traces the curve of my ass. "You know, there are ways a woman can have two men at once, if you ever think you could handle it. More efficient—and I believe even more satisfying—that way."

I shiver at the thought, licking my lips.

Watching my reaction, Jostein squeezes my ass in turn and then skims my back opening. The nerves there light up with a flare of sensation like nothing I've ever felt.

"A pity we didn't think of that earlier," he says in a low voice that melts me. "It'll have to wait for the next time."

My noise of agreement comes out like a mewling more than anything else. Iko groans and bucks up to meet me.

I sway between the thrust of his cock and the provocative pressure of Jostein's fingers. I'd have expected to find myself too spent to reach my peak again at all quickly, but the pleasure swells inside me so rapidly I'm dizzy with it.

I run my fingers over Iko's chest, loosening the ties on his shirt and delving to the taut skin beneath. Match him kiss for wild kiss. Hiss a breath through my teeth when Jostein works a finger right inside me from the opposite end, aided by the slickness of my own arousal.

"We're going to give you everything you've needed," Iko promises in an increasingly ragged voice. "Everything you deserve."

He clutches my thigh as he picks up his pace, slamming me down to meet him and flicking his thumb across my clit. My fingernails dig into his sides, and he groans. "Fuck, you're too delicious. Come with me, Spitfire. Come with me all the way."

He swirls his thumb around my clit again with an even more forceful thrust. Jostein echoes the motion from behind.

With a whimper, I soar up and over my peak.

My eyes roll up, my vision briefly whiting out. Iko's breath stutters, his hips jerking, and then he's pulling me down over him, nestling my head against the crook of his shoulder.

Jostein withdraws his hand with one final caress of my back. He leans over to kiss my cheek.

I feel as much as see Iko gaze up at his friend through the dimness. "She is *our* woman. We can give her that much more if we're in this together."

He says it as a statement, but his muscles tense beneath me with a momentary uneasiness.

Jostein answers with a soft smile. "Our woman, for as long as she wants the both of us."

I barely restrain a snort at the idea that *my* interest would be the deciding factor.

As if he senses my skepticism, Iko cups my face. His voice comes out more tender than usual. "You're the only woman I can see myself ever wanting again, Signy. No one else has ever come close to matching you."

I don't know how to answer that statement of devotion except with a lingering kiss. He kisses me back just as ardently.

As I start to peel myself off Iko, a familiar voice carries through the tent wall.

"Signy?"

It's Landric—looking for me, apparently. His tone sounds concerned.

Iko grumbles a curse, and I snatch at my clothes. Jostein yanks up his trousers.

We emerge from the tent probably looking like people who were doing exactly what we were doing. I'm still straightening my tunic, vaguely aware of my well-rumpled hair. Iko's shirt hangs partly open, and Jostein is simply carrying his rather than pulling it back on. As if he *wants* our recent activities to be obvious.

When the squad leader folds his arms over his chest, staring through the forest, I get the impression he's staking a claim, even if it doesn't exclude his friend.

Landric has passed us by, wandering between the tents. I clear my throat, my cheeks prickling with a sudden heat. "I'm over here."

He spins on his heel and then simply stops, taking in the three of us. The heat in my face flares, but I keep my chin high and my gaze steady.

A hint of a flush creeps over Landric's face in turn, but to give him credit, he doesn't avert his gaze or go storming off. "I didn't mean to interrupt anything."

"That's all right," Iko says, draping his arm across my shoulders in a possessive gesture of his own. "This lovely woman has been well taken care of. You wanted to talk to her?"

Landric fumbles with his words. "I—yes—there—" He pauses, swallows, and seems to gather himself. "I wanted to speak with you before going to the officers, since this is really your rebellion. I had an idea for the next time we confront the Darium army."

A hint of a smile touches his lips. "You could say your trick with the lissweld pollen inspired me."

CHAPTER SIXTEEN

Signy

Captain Amalia grimaces as she smears the yellowish green algae over her dark skin. "You're sure this part is absolutely necessary?"

Landric's mouth twists apologetically. "Unless you like the idea of getting stung by a horde of wasps."

"No, I suppose I'd prefer to avoid that outcome." She shakes her head. "Well, even if the stings don't do the job well enough, the stink should keep the Darium soldiers far enough away they won't be able to murder us."

Her dry tone and the ridiculousness of the situation shock a laugh from my throat despite the tension balled tight inside me.

I restrain a grimace of my own as I dip my hand into the murky pond. The odor that rises off the water makes me think of rotting fish. A shudder runs through me as I slather more algae across my arms and onto my cheeks.

But it'll be worth it if it means we can carve a bigger hole in the Darium army. At least the summer day is warm enough that the dampness isn't unpleasant too.

Iko uses a stick to swirl the film that coats the surface of the water, his own tan skin already yellowed by drying algae. "Hard to believe anything else can live in this mess."

"I don't think much does," Landric says, straightening up. He's streaked the slimy stuff even through his coppery hair, but somehow he's still handsome with his eagerness to share his knowledge brightening his expression. "The harvesters cultivate these ponds around the marl tree forests so they have easy access to the algae when they need it. I don't think they care about much else."

As we step back from the pond to give more of our allies a chance to slather themselves in the protective vegetation, Jostein shakes his head. "I wonder how the nobles on their estates would feel if they knew how much of a stink surrounds their fine furniture."

Landric chuckles. "That's why marlwood is so expensive —dealing with the damned wasps. But I don't think the people who buy the products made from it give it much thought beyond knowing that type of wood is a valuable commodity."

He knows because of the work his family does—because of how he's helped his merchant parents with their business. When he presented his plan to me and then the officers last night, he explained that it'd occurred to him there was a marlwood forest within a few hours' march of our current camp.

I examine my limbs for any patches of bare skin I might have missed. "What happens if the algae doesn't ward the wasps off enough and they sting us too?"

Landric's voice softens. "That shouldn't happen. Not when they'll have plenty of other targets to take out their annoyance on. But just a few stings will only hurt a lot and slow down your reactions. It takes several for full paralysis to set in. The only deaths I've ever heard of were unprepared folk stumbling into a stretch of marl trees and stirring up an awful lot of the wasps. They don't even come out from their tunnels unless they're disturbed."

Of course, we're going to be purposefully provoking the insects from their preferred home just beneath the bark of the trees. But I guess marlwood wouldn't be a commodity at all if the harvesters couldn't cut down trees to harvest it without being stung to death.

I'm not sure how well-known marlwood is in our neighboring realms, let alone all the way to Dariu. It's possible someone in the Darium force is aware of its unique relationship with the wasps. But it seems unlikely they'd also be aware of exactly where the local supply happens to come from.

As we tramp around the edge of the forest, I breathe through my mouth to avoid the worst of the stench. At least we're all in this smelly situation together.

Over where the woodland comes up on the nearby road, there's a stretch with about a quarter mile of more peaceful trees—cultivated purposefully so that travelers through this area don't accidentally set off a wasp attack. We've removed the signs warning of the marl trees beyond. Several of our soldiers are setting up tents and scattering equipment so it looks as if we were using this part of the forest as a camp rather than an ambush.

The Darium army won't be quite as quick to charge after us now that we've played one trick on them. We need them to think they've caught us rather than that we welcomed the fight.

Another soldier lopes through the trees and tips his head to Captain Amalia. We've been leaving traces of our journey so the Darium forces can track us down, making the evidence look as accidental as we're able to.

After yesterday's confrontation, none of us has any doubt that High Commander Livius and his underlings will be eager for vengeance.

Our last sentry to arrive reported that the army was marching this way, only a couple of hours distant. I peer through the trees, hoping the man who stayed back to play a peddler walking the road will come out of his encounter with the Darium force in one piece.

He has to let the soldiers think they've bullied him into admitting he saw us hiding in these woods. With the grace of the gods, they'll be in enough of a hurry to follow our trail that they simply toss him aside once he's coughed up the information.

I check my sword at my side as if the algae might have stolen it when I wasn't looking, my pulse beating faster. We had a huge victory yesterday. Today's scheme isn't even my plan—I'm not responsible for how it turns out.

But I'm here in the thick of it. And none of the other people around me would be here if I hadn't lit the first spark of rebellion.

I sit down next to rather than on a bed roll, not wanting to risk contaminating it with the stink, and will my nerves to settle as well as I can. We can't act until the Darium army reaches us. There's nothing to do at the moment but wait.

Landric sinks onto the ground next to me, his eyes equally alert. Jostein and Iko have gathered with a few squadmates around Captain Amalia. As my gaze lingers on them, taking in Jostein's assured stance and Iko's brilliant grin, Landric glances over at me.

He must be able to tell where I'm looking. His voice comes out low and even. "What's going on between you and them… it's more than just physical, isn't it?"

I swallow hard, the motion bringing back an aftertaste of the mirewort Jostein passed to me earlier this morning. To make sure there are no unintended consequences from our passionate interlude. *For now*, he said as he set the packet in my hand, with a gleam in his bright blue eyes as if he could imagine a future when pregnancy would be welcome rather than a mistake.

The memory of that moment and of Landric finding us last night sends an awkward flush through my body. "I don't see how it's any of your business."

Landric winces. "I know it's not. I know… I have a long way to go before you'll really trust me. And you deserve to be happy."

I raise an eyebrow. "I feel like there's a 'but' coming."

"Not really." His gaze drops to the twigs and pebbles scattered on the forest floor around his feet. "This isn't how I'd have wanted to look—or smell—when putting this out there, but it seems like I'd better say it now or I'll lose any chance at all. I already lost so many when you were right there in front of me in town."

Is he trying to present himself as an alternate suitor? My previous flush turns prickly beneath my skin. "If you're saying that I should entertain your interest over theirs—"

"No," Landric says quickly, his head jerking back up so he can meet my eyes. "That wouldn't be fair of me. But if it isn't a competition between them, maybe… maybe you'd be willing to consider me alongside them."

My breath snags in my throat. I don't know how to answer him when he's looking at me so earnestly, when all our tangled, painful history still hangs over us.

He means it right now. I don't think he would have a couple of weeks ago. How quickly could his affections shift all over again?

I still don't trust him. So why does my heart thump even faster at his proposition?

Before I have to respond to him or myself, a short whistle pierces the air. My stance tenses, rising up so I'm braced on my feet.

The army is almost on us. Any moment now…

The seconds pass by with the rustle of the leaves overhead and the stench of dried algae seeping into my nose. I've almost sat down again, thinking it was a false alarm, when one of the sentries posted at the edge of the forest comes running into our midst.

"The Darium army—they've found us! We've got to get out of here!"

He yells loud enough for his voice to carry all the way to the road behind him—which is the point. Let the enemy soldiers think they're falling on us unexpectedly, that they've driven us into a panic.

We scramble to our feet, panic not at all difficult to feign when all those swords and lances are bearing down on us. At least the trees will shelter us from distant arrows.

Landric grasps my arm with a quick squeeze, fear flickering through his expression and vanishing beneath a firming of determination. A thunder of stomping feet reverberates through the trees as the Darium army barrels toward us.

All of us take off for the deeper forest. We need them to see us fleeing but not quite catch up with us until we're amid the marl trees.

Taunting shouts ring out behind us. The high commander's voice booms out in the same contemptuous tone as yesterday. "You won't escape us now, vermin. We'll stamp you all out like the rats you are."

The stampede of footsteps sounds from either side of us —the Darium soldiers doing their best to surround us, coming up along the edges of this patch of forest where they can run faster on the un-treed ground.

I push myself faster and spot the mottled gray bark of the first marl trees up ahead.

A crossbow bolt zings through the air to slam into a trunk. Someone farther behind me cries out.

I hurtle into the midst of the marl trees alongside my comrades, all of us whipping out our weapons. Whacking the bark on one tree with the flat of my sword, I kick the next nearest trunk at the same time before dashing onward. All around me, bodies and blades thud against the precious trees.

And then the buzzing starts.

A fierce hum swells in the air as hundreds of tiny red-and-brown bodies spew from little holes in the tree bark. The angry insects shoot right past me, raising the hairs on the back of my neck but not pausing to aim their stingers at me.

They careen straight toward the unprotected soldiers storming into our midst.

The wasps fly at uncovered hands, at the gaps in helms and around collars, as penetrating as the lissweld pollen but ten times more vicious. The figures in their skeletal uniforms who barged into the forest break out into a horrifically ridiculous dance, shaking and slapping as they try to fend off the miniscule attackers.

As their larger enemies, we can't just stand back and watch. The Veldunian soldiers among us launch themselves at the Darium force, cutting down our opponents while they're distracted by the wasps.

Some of the Darium soldiers have already crumpled over, the toxin in the stingers numbing their bodies. I can't quite stomach stabbing those people in my inexpert way while they're so defenseless, but I knock off their helms, giving the wasps better access. Welts are swelling around their necks and mouths.

One woman lurches forward with a jab of her sword toward Landric, who has his back turned to her as he shoves away another soldier. My heart lurches. I swing my own sword with all the strength I used to put into my axe when I chopped wood at my old cabin.

The blade slams down on her wrist and severs it from her body so abruptly my jaw goes slack.

Landric whirls around at the woman's groan. She slumps over, yanking the stump of her arm closer to her body, trying to huddle against more wasps descending on her.

My childhood friend blinks and looks at me with a mix of shock and relief. "Thank you."

A sudden guffaw tumbles out of me. "Thank *you* for this fantastic plan."

The cries echoing between the trees are all triumphant now as the Darium soldiers lie broken or dash away in another retreat. We've won the day once more.

I can only imagine how much more furious the survivors will be when they descend on us next. But that's a problem for another day.

CHAPTER SEVENTEEN

Signy

L aughter bounces across the water along the shore of the vast lake at the foot of the mountains. My comrades slosh around, thigh- to chest-deep in the cool water, rinsing the remains of the stinking algae from our skin and clothes.

I wobble on the rocky lake floor, and Iko grasps my arm to steady me. He aims a grin at me, looking twice as roguish with his blond hair slicked back and darkened with the water. "Need a little help washing up?"

I pat my face. "Did I miss a spot?"

"There's a little in your hair…"

He guides me to lean backward and swishes my hair in the water with unexpected gentleness. But of course he takes a moment to stroke his fingers right over my scalp in a provocative caress.

As he pulls me upright, my cheeks warm. "Aiming to be thorough?"

He chuckles, his hand on my waist. "Nothing wrong with having a little fun at the same time."

At my teasingly disgruntled sound, he leans closer, lowering his voice. "We hit the Darium army with quite a blow. It'll take at least a couple of days for them to recover. I think tonight we should look forward to a lot more fun."

I arch my eyebrows at him, though a flush has spread all across my skin despite the cool water. "Oh, do you?"

He hums meaningfully. "And I'd imagine Jostein would agree."

With another flash of a grin, he dips his head to claim a quick kiss. Apparently he doesn't care who knows how our relationship has developed.

And maybe there's no reason to worry. Most of our companions are too busy reveling in relief to pay attention, and the few who've glanced our way simply smile with fond amusement.

No more sneering comments. No more disdainful glowers.

No one here seems to care anymore about the fact that my godlen didn't reward my dedication sacrifice. I've created something so much bigger, so much better than anything the gift I prayed for would have allowed.

I take in the broader sprawl of our camp in a semi-circle around the lake. My gaze seems to skip across the fields to the south, as if given an inexplicable nudge.

I frown, but Iko grasps my hand to tug me over to the shore, and my momentary uneasiness fades. There's nothing over there. I'm just worn out from the intense day—the intense *week*—we've managed to survive.

As Iko and I wade to shore, I peer through the rippling water at the rocky terrain. I have to lift my foot higher to clamber over a dark gap between the stones.

My attention rises to the mountain looming right at the

far side of the lake. I can pick out several dark crevices along its base too.

"There are caves broken into the rocks," I comment. "I wonder how far and how deep they run. Back at Feldan, there were passages all under the hills and the town. Some people used them for storerooms."

Now those openings will be buried under ash and charred wood. I hope no one tried to hide in one of the natural cellars and found themselves unable to shift the door to climb back out.

A shudder passes through me at the thought, but Iko scans the landscape with a curious air. "We should do some exploring once we've dried off. It's always good to know what we have to work with."

We rub ourselves down with blankets and spread them out to dry. The summer air turns cool across my still-damp clothes, but it's more refreshing than chilly with the sun beaming down on us.

Memories of those narrow crevices around the town nibble at my mind. I knit my brow. I can almost see... "I think if we had enough time to prepare, maybe there's a way to use—"

My gaze slides over the landscape around us, and that unnerving sensation hits me again, harder. As if my eyes have been propelled away through a will not my own.

My body tenses, my voice dying in my mouth. Iko catches my reaction immediately. "What's wrong?"

I swallow thickly, my stomach twisting with a sudden nausea. "I'm not sure. Something just feels... strange. You don't see anything around here, do you?"

Iko considers the mountain range and then the fields nearby. Watching his expression, I catch a slight tick. His shoulders stiffen too.

"I think—there's some kind of magic at work." He raises his voice. "Major Arlo! Captain Amalia! We need to—"

He never gets to finish his suggestion. At his first shouts, dozens of heads swivel around all across our campsite—and the illusion breaks.

Stampeding figures waver into view all across the fields around us. There must be hundreds of them coming from the north, more from the east and west, every direction except the towering mountains.

As they charge toward us, they shed the drapings of greenish fabric that helped the illusionary magic conceal them. The skeletal uniforms of the Darium soldiers stand out starkly against the grassy terrain.

Their blades flash. Bows draw back with arrows launched into the air.

I cry out and scramble backward, but I don't really know where to run. The camp turns into a teeming mass of panic, officers shouting for us to grab our weapons, curses and gasps of terror mingling with the orders.

I manage to snatch up my short sword, as much good as it might do me. Arrows hurtle into our midst, toppling a man just a few paces from where I'm standing, a woman I shared breakfast with this morning.

How did the Darium forces regroup and find us so quickly? How much magic must it have taken to hide so many of them?

Even in my horror, I spot the dark green uniforms amid the Darium standard. Duke Berengar's livery. He's had a hand in this assault—he's helped them plot their counterattack.

It doesn't make any sense that most of them have come from nearly the opposite direction from where we last encountered the Darium forces. We only arrived at the lake a couple of hours ago.

Unless these are other soldiers. Has the duke been rallying the squadrons already stationed here in Velduny, gathering them to launch an offensive at our flanks?

It could have been even worse if they'd caught us on totally open ground.

And is that a woman in an orange robe, vividly bright at the back of the swarm? As soon as I've noticed her, I pick out a few more people in similar attire at the rear of the charge.

As I scramble away, a chill consumes my gut. They're devouts of Inganne, no doubt from the temple that glitters beneath the sunlight to the west. With the godlen's affinity with imagination and play, dedicats seeking gifts of illusion often turn to her.

Did the Darium soldiers force them to contribute their magic, or did they ally themselves freely with our enemy?

It hardly matters now. The soldiers close in around us, plowing into the rebels at the edges of the camp. Blood sprays and bodies slump—mostly on our side.

Captain Amalia's voice splits through the bellows and shrieks of the fray. "Up the mountain! Take the higher ground!"

I whirl around, and Iko is there, gripping my elbow. As we dash around the shoreline toward the rocky slope, Jostein barrels past us on his horse, his sword swinging. A protest snags in my throat with the urge to call him back, to beg him to flee with us.

But the loyal squad leader would never put his own safety first. He'll stay to the bitter end, helping all of us who can escape make it to safety, just like he did for me that first night in Feldan.

Iko tugs me onward. "If anyone can make it through this mess, it's Jostein. He'll focus better if he knows I've gotten you out of the line of fire."

How far do we need to run for that? As we clamber up

the steepening slope, more arrows pelt the frantic crowd around us. Another comrade falls, and another.

I have to dodge a body that tumbles down the incline right in front of me, blood blooming from the shaft piercing her chest.

My groping hands clutch at wizened trees and spears of stone to speed my climb. The rough surfaces scrape at my palms, but I barely notice the sting. My lungs burn with the exertion alongside the growing ache in my calves.

Finally, no more arrows whistle into our midst. Iko urges me a little higher, up to a narrow plateau where we can stand somewhat steadily.

A few dozen of our allies have already arrived there, more gathering above and below to stare down the slope at the camp we were forced to abandon.

Corpses in the plain clothes of rebels scatter the field around the edge of the lake and the lower reaches of the mountain. More bloody red meets my eyes than the green of the grass or the gray of the rocks.

The Darium soldiers and their helpers pick their way between the bodies, peering up at the remainder of our resistance. I can't help looking around me, taking in our dwindled battalion too.

I'm not sure even half of us survived the onslaught. Where's Jostein? What happened to Landric?

My pulse races for several panicked seconds before I spot Jostein walking beside his horse along the slope, down by the lowest of our surviving allies. Blood darkens his sleeve and chest, but I can't tell how much of it if any is his. He's striding along steadily enough to reassure me.

Landric's hair gleams beneath the late afternoon sun where he's poised off to the side of our little plateau. I can't make out much more of him, but he is at least standing.

There's no sign of High Commander Livius with his multiply-plumed helm. This isn't his army at all.

A Darium soldier with a single-plumed helmet marking him as a lesser officer marches to the bottom of the slope. As he studies our huddled forms, his lips curl into a sneer.

"You enjoy your mountainside," he calls up to us in an equally mocking tone. "Our colleagues are already on their way to join us. I'm sure the high commander will want to have a part in executing the rest of you."

Their colleagues—what's left of the army we've tricked to many of their deaths twice now. Yes, they will be angry. My legs wobble under me.

It seems the Darium force isn't foolhardy enough to clamber after us and continue the battle with us very literally on higher ground. They draw back beyond the scene of the slaughter, some of the soldiers setting up tents of their own while others remain on guard.

My fellow rebels stir uneasily around me. Muffled sobs reach my ears from somewhere beyond my view. Every face my gaze catches on has fallen, shadowed with grief and fear.

I think we lost one of our captains in the attack. Only four of them have stepped off to the side with Major Arlo to confer, although I'm relieved to see Captain Amalia is among them.

I look down at the mass of fallen bodies again, and my stomach clenches up. So many dead.

So many who were only here because I called for this uprising. Because I claimed we could win.

After those two victories, I really believed we had a chance. That we could keep winning, over and over, until the Darium empire was beaten.

Who's beaten now?

I sink down to the ground, drawing my legs up in front

of me. Iko follows, his expression tensing with concern. "Are you all right? If you're injured—"

I shake my head, too choked up to speak. No, *I'm* perfectly fine, at least in body. Unlike hundreds of the soldiers and civilians I rallied around me.

I led them to their deaths. And the Darium soldiers intend to slaughter all the rest of us—and who knows how many total innocents as well—in punishment.

Who in the realms did I think I was? I *knew* it could end like this, I knew I might be reaching too far, and I dragged so many people down with me anyway.

Someone pushes through the crowd toward us. I can't quite bring myself to raise my head, but I know Jostein's voice as soon as he speaks, breathless with relief. "You both made it."

He kneels down, touching my hair. "We can recover from this, Signy. We won't let them catch us unprepared again."

But even as his last word fades in the air, the major and the captains march over to address the rest of us survivors. I've never seen Major Arlo's face so grim.

"Good people of Velduny," he says in a low but resonant tone that carries over all of us. "We've put up a good fight. We've done more damage to the Darium forces than most would have imagined possible. But in light of the losses we just suffered and the challenges ahead... I feel it's time to discuss surrender."

Chapter Eighteen

Jostein

As I watch the officers in their hushed twilight conference, my jaw clenches. Every particle of my being itches to be in there with them, speaking against the surrender, laying out plans of my own. Showing how we can lead the people who've believed in this cause to a better outcome.

But I don't actually know what plan would get us out of this mess. Maybe that's why I'm over here with the infantry and the civilians, waiting in the growing gloom to hear someone else determine our fate.

Anger smolders inside me despite the increasingly hopeless atmosphere. We can't give up now. We can't let all the people who fell to Darium swords and arrows today have died in vain.

It's hard to keep up my own hope when I stalk back to where I left Signy sitting with Iko, though. Her head has drooped even farther than when I last saw her, her dark hair drifting across her shoulders and the knees she's hugging. Her slumped shoulders look unnervingly fragile.

I've watched this woman challenge an entire squadron alone. I've seen her fight tooth and nail for her home when no one else was willing to.

It always seemed like the strength she radiated was something innate and unshakeable. But she's obviously shaken now.

While I've been gone, Landric has come over to sit with her too, keeping a careful distance opposite Iko. The same anguish I feel is etched all across his face.

I don't know all the details of what went on between them in the past, but he clearly cares about her. Somehow that both annoys me and reassures me.

This magnificent woman needs all the caring she can get. All the caring she was denied for so long before she took up this mission.

I crouch down on the uneven ground next to Iko, turned to face Signy, but she doesn't look up. It's my friend who acknowledges my presence first. "Any news from the bigwigs?"

I shake my head. "They're still discussing our options. Trying to come up with an offer that'll save as many lives as possible, I'd imagine."

What's to stop the Darium force from slaughtering us all, really? It'll be easy enough once the rest of their army arrives, which may only be a matter of hours from now.

"Too many people already died," Signy murmurs in a rough voice.

My heart wrenches. I'm amazed that we made it so long without more initial casualties. She's never had to face the realities of warfare. She has no idea how much blood ends up being shed even to win.

"We all knew what we were risking when we took up the

cause," I say, as steadily as I can. "I know none of my colleagues would have regretted making the gamble for what we stood to gain. What we *still* stand to gain."

A choked guffaw sputters out of her. "Still? We've lost. It took them just minutes to murder half of our comrades. They're only holding back from cutting down the rest of us until we pose even less of a threat than we already do."

Landric's stance tenses. "Which means we have time. We started with less than we have now. We started with just the four of us."

"Taking on a guard post, not an entire army."

Iko makes a dismissive sound. "It wasn't manpower that won the battles before this one. They always had us outnumbered. Our wits made the difference."

"Until they didn't anymore."

I reach out to graze my fingers over Signy's hair. She lifts her head just enough to peer at me between the strands. So much sorrow shadows her normally vibrant eyes that my throat constricts.

I want to tell her how we can win the war after all. I want to point the way and command everyone onto the path of victory.

But that has never been my actual role since I was first drawn into this quest. Signy was the driving force.

I was the one who recognized the potential in her. Who could see how much *she* could accomplish.

Because it's all I have, I lean into the one certainty my gift gave me. "We've had a harsh setback, but that doesn't mean this is over. We've faced setbacks before and come back stronger. You've always seen the way through, and I know you can again. All these people are here because you inspired them. You inspired *me*."

Signy swipes her hand across her mouth. "I inspired

hundreds of them to their deaths. Just because I couldn't stand to let the Darium empire keep lording it over us."

Ah. It isn't just grief but guilt tying her into knots.

I caress her hair again, summoning all the conviction and authority I can bring to bear. "The deaths today aren't your fault. Signy, you're surrounded by hundreds of trained soldiers, and not one of us caught on to the threat in time to prevent the attack. They used skills and tactics we didn't anticipate, and that's on us. How could you expect to be prepared when not even Major Arlo was?"

As she grimaces, Iko picks up my thread with a squeeze of her shoulder. "And you were the first to realize something was wrong. If you hadn't said something to me, they might have gotten even closer before anyone sounded the alarm. Even more lives would have been lost."

Landric shifts his position as if he wants to reach out to her too, but he holds himself back. "The Darium forces were killing Veldunian citizens long before you ever took up this rebellion. The only difference is that we've finally been making them pay. We finally have the chance to get rid of them completely."

"How?" Signy demands. "There's no lissweld or marlwood wasps here. We're stuck up a mountain with an army at the foot."

A crooked smile crosses my lips. "You haven't given yourself the opportunity to believe there's a way out of this. If you can find that faith again, I have total confidence that more strategies will come to you."

Iko perks up. "You were starting to tell me an idea down by the lake when you noticed the illusionary magic. You'd already thought of another way to turn the tables on them, hadn't you?"

A brief glimmer lights in Signy's eyes. She opens her mouth and closes it again, the spark fading.

I lean forward, knowing that if I accomplish anything tonight, it has to be fanning that ember back into flame. "What? What were you picturing?"

"I—I don't know. That was before we were stuck up here. Before we lost so many people. We'd need time... It'd have been a lot to pull off even before."

"We're not doing anything yet," I say firmly. "You're not insisting on anything. You're just telling us what you imagined. Let us judge whether it's worth pursuing. That part won't be on you."

Signy wets her lips. For a second, I think she's going to refuse again.

Then she lifts her chin a little higher. "There are caves in the mountain, under the lake—maybe all around here. The terrain around Feldan is like that too. A layer of soil over lots of rock, with crevices and passages all through it..."

She glances at Landric, who's watching her avidly. "Do you remember when we were little kids—when there was that cave-in by the old cistern? Rafe and his sister fell in."

Landric's gaze goes distant with the recollection. "The ceiling of a cave under the field collapsed. Rafe bashed his head and his leg—he never thought or walked the same after that. Maika nearly died from the bleeding."

"A fall like that does a lot of damage." Signy's head turns so she can gaze through the thickening dusk toward the remnants of her former home. "Those caves ran all through Feldan and out into the nearby fields as well as the forest... If we could thin or crack the ceilings so they'd be on the verge of collapsing and then lure the Darium soldiers there to fall... But I don't know if that would be possible even if we had days to work on it."

Landric springs to his feet. "I've talked to at least a couple of people who have gifts that could help set it up. I'll make sure they're still with us and see who else I can find who'd be able to pitch in."

Signy stiffens. "You don't have to—"

He fixes her with a look so intense it sets off every jealous impulse in my body. "I want to. It's a fantastic plan." His gaze lifts to me. "Isn't it?"

"We don't have enough of the pieces pulled together for me to evaluate with my gift," I say. "But if we can pull it off, I think it'd be exactly what we need."

As Landric hustles off, Signy's gaze follows him. I think I see a faint flush in her cheeks.

I shove down the jealousy and focus on the part of me that wants to see this woman adored. The remark manages to come out in a casual tone. "He's awfully devoted to you."

Her attention jerks back to me with a twist of her mouth. "He's just—he feels bad about not standing up for me sooner. He's trying to make it up to me so he doesn't have to feel guilty."

Iko chuckles. "I think it's more than that. It just took him much longer to recognize what an incredible woman you are than it did the two of us. His fault for being late to the party."

Signy gives a soft snort at his phrasing, but the hint of a blush remains.

I pick my words carefully. "He has been a valuable and loyal member of our rebellion from the very start. The four of us worked well together."

She stares at me for a moment. "What are you saying?"

I lift my shoulders in a slight shrug. "We obviously have more pressing concerns at the moment. But as far as I'm concerned, if you felt you could accept all the devotion three of us could offer you rather than two... I wouldn't want to hold you back."

Iko elbows me. "Hey, now I'll look bad if I say I want her all for ourselves."

Signy's expression has shifted to something somewhere between incredulity and amusement. "Is that what you'd have said?"

Iko grins at her, his posture relaxing. "You know, when we first met, I might have said I'd rather have you all just for me. But there's something pretty fantastic about a collaboration. I liked seeing how much you enjoyed the two of us together. Three… that could be even more spectacular."

There's no doubt now that Signy's tan skin has reddened. She ducks her head in momentary embarrassment and then pushes herself to her feet. "Well, none of it matters if we're all facing execution tomorrow."

Her gaze slides toward the cluster of officers farther along the mountainside. "It doesn't matter what brilliant plan we come up with if the major and the captains don't agree."

I give her hand a quick squeeze. "Then we'll have to be very convincing."

It takes even less time than I expect before our comrades begin to gather around the three of us—some of my fellow soldiers looking to me and Iko with questioning expressions, some of the ordinary citizens studying Signy.

"I heard you might have a way we can knock the Darium bastards back on their asses," one of them says cautiously.

Before this afternoon's massacre, I'd have expected Signy to hold her head high with a daring smile and assure them we're heading toward another victory. Now, I'm not entirely surprised to see her hesitate, even if it pains me. My attempt at a pep talk hasn't been enough to fully restore her confidence.

If she needs more, I can provide it. She isn't alone anymore—and she needs to see that the people she's brought together are still willing to fight for our freedom despite today's tragedy.

"We might have an opportunity to shatter the entire Darium force," I say. "We can't back down now, not when we've made so much progress. They believe they have the upper hand again—it's the perfect time to upset the balance."

A few of our companions look nervous, but most draw themselves straighter with determined expressions. They've watched friends and neighbors die today. They've had a stark reminder of the brutality we've spent the past three centuries enduring.

To drive the point home, I gesture toward the Darium camp beyond the lake. "They want to kill all of us. I say we spill their blood instead. Every Darium soldier we take down is one fewer who can torment the rest of us in years to come."

It's possible none of us will survive the next day, but if we hit back hard enough, we might still carve the way to a better future. All of Velduny will be hearing about the stand we've taken.

All we can hope for is to weaken the Darium presence in our country as much as possible, regardless of what fate we meet.

The murmurs of anticipation that pass through the growing crowd around us seem to invigorate Signy. She tosses back her hair and sets her hands on her hips. "I started us on this path, and I'm going to keep fighting until the end. You all have to make the decisions that are right for you. But I'd be honored to have you taking on those pricks alongside me."

As several voices call out in support, Landric hustles back to us with a dozen figures trailing behind him. His face has lit up with enthusiasm.

He's that happy to be playing this role—to be helping

orchestrate the rebellion, to be showing Signy she isn't beaten. Seeing it, I can't resent his interest in her one bit.

"I think we could pull it off," he says to us in a hushed voice. "We've got people skilled with rock work, construction, carving… I have a few asking around to see if there are other talents that could contribute. The hardest part might be setting off the cave-ins at the right time. We'd want the ground to hold steady enough at first for plenty of the soldiers to get into the area, right?"

Signy nods, her expression turning thoughtful. "We'll need to create a big impact, some kind of shock to the ground. Explosives?"

She glances at Iko, whose grin turns sly. "You know I won't pass up the chance to see what I can throw together to stir things up."

A cleared throat brings my head snapping around.

Major Arlo and the captains have approached our expanding huddle. The major frowns at us. "What's going on over here? If we're going to negotiate as peaceful a surrender as possible, we can't be agitating the Darium forces any further."

He holds himself with an assurance I can't help admiring. Ever since I was a kid, I dreamed of taking on a role like his, leading hundreds of soldiers in defense of our country. All my training tells me to stand down and follow orders.

That's not enough, though. If I want to lead my fellow citizens on the right path, I have to start now, when it could make the most difference.

No, this plan isn't mine. But part of me knew all the way back at twelve years old that sometimes the best leadership doesn't come from seeing the route forward but getting everyone else on it once a visionary has pointed out the way.

Every bit of my gift is telling me that the people we've

assembled, the people I've believed in from the start, can tackle this final challenge.

I square my shoulders. "We're not ready to surrender, sir."

The major's jaw ticks. "It's hardly up to you. We've fought hard, but we've been overwhelmed—"

"We can turn the tables on them again," Signy breaks in, with so much of her old passion that my heart leaps to see it. "We're putting together a strategy—if we get started on it right away, it could completely cripple the Darium forces."

One of the captains steps in. "It's our job to decide whether the risks are worth the potential gains."

I fold my arms over my chest. "This isn't just an army. This is a rebellion. None of us are following the rules anymore. If the people here want to keep fighting rather than giving up, I think your options are to do whatever you can to make that work—or give your own surrender."

The captain's gaze sharpens into a glare, but Amalia pushes past him. "My squad leader has a point." She takes in the people who've gathered around us. "Do you really want to keep going?"

This time, there's no hesitation, no uncertainty. The voices rise up in a rush of defiance. "We have to keep fighting."

"We're in this until the end."

"Let's take as many of those assholes down as we can."

When my captain catches my eyes, I catch a glint of pride in hers. I doubt she was ever keen on the idea of surrendering. "Then I say we hear about this plan of yours."

I set my hand on my lover's shoulder. "Signy saw how it could happen."

CHAPTER NINETEEN

Signy

I watch the next group of rebels depart through the night with a brief wave of farewell. As they slink along the mountainside through the darkness, heading well past the view of the Darium guards before they descend and hurry north toward Feldan, my stomach knots.

I can't shake the feeling that I should be going with them. That I should have joined the first bunch of resistors who took most of our remaining horses to race off toward the town so they'd have as much time as possible to work their gifts.

But I don't have any gift at all. My contribution was coming up with the plan. The best I can do now is keep everyone's spirits up to see it through.

Jostein approaches with a rasp of his boots over the uneven rock. He stops beside me, tucking his arm around my waist in a gesture that feels so natural now it sends a quiver of giddiness through me.

We've known each other for a little over a week, but

we've spent nearly every moment of that together. And with each of those moments, no matter how fraught, he's proven that he sees me as so much more of a true partner than any of my previous, fleeting flings did.

His thumb strokes over my back in a gentle caress. "How are you holding up?"

I let out a short guffaw. "I'm not on the front lines. I hope the stone workers and the rest we sent ahead aren't finding the task too much."

Jostein hums. "I didn't ask about them. I asked about you. You've taken on a lot of responsibility from the beginning, and now isn't any different."

A lump forms in my throat at his recognition of the pressure I'm feeling. I'm not sure I'd have dared to speak this plan, let alone attempt it, if it wasn't for the squad leader's encouragement earlier.

I lean into his touch, accepting the comfort he's offering. "I'm nervous, but I'm not letting it get to me. Even if this goes wrong, we'll end things taking as many of them with us as we can."

"Have you gotten any rest?"

I nod. "I managed to doze for a couple of hours after the first group left. No more time now—Captain Amalia said the rest of us should leave after the next bell."

Jostein turns me toward him. "No matter what happens, this is better than waiting on a mountainside to be executed. You gave us this chance, rebel maiden."

He dips his head to kiss me. The heat of his lips lights up my body with a tender heat that's a balm on my frayed nerves.

At the sound of more footsteps, we ease apart. Landric is walking over to join us, with a slightly apologetic dip of his head. There's an almost feverish brightness to his eyes that I can tell at once has nothing to do with jealousy.

"I think I can strengthen our strategy," he says.

The intensity in his voice combined with his expression makes my heart skip a beat. "How?"

He tilts his head toward the few remaining lights of the Darium camp below the hill. "Rupert's with the soldiers. I don't know whether he asked to lead the guards the duke contributed or if the Darium officers insisted that Duke Berengar send his son as a sign of full commitment, but it doesn't really matter. He knows me; he can vouch that I've generally been on his side."

A chill trickles through my gut. "But you spoke to him before about joining the rebellion."

Landric shrugs. "Only vaguely and briefly. He thinks highly of himself and his sway—he'd be happy to assume that his comments persuaded me away from any rebellious ideas. He'll at least be able to speak up for me with the Darium force in a way he wouldn't anyone else among us."

"Why would he need to speak up for you?" Jostein asks in an even tone.

Landric's stance tenses as he straightens his posture. "I'll approach their camp after the rest of you have had a chance to make it to Feldan. Around the first light of the morning? We were worried they'd notice our disappearance and send just a smaller force to track us down, and our efforts wouldn't injure very many of them. I can tell them that I saw my old neighbors and their new comrades heading toward Feldan, and they boasted about how they have many more allies who'll be coming to meet them there shortly."

Understanding unfurls inside me. "So they'll see us as a greater threat."

"Exactly. Hopefully I can convince them without outright saying it that they should wait to march on you until the rest of the army has joined them so they'll have the benefit of full numbers, and then we can take them all down together. And that should give you more time to carry out the plan."

It could help. It could help quite a bit, if he plays the part well.

But Jostein puts the concern that's constricted my chest into words. "They might cut *you* down simply for carrying the message. They're not going to let you walk off after you give your report."

Landric lifts his shoulders in another shrug, though this one looks stiffer than the first. "It is what it is. I won't be able to contribute much to the plan otherwise. You're all risking your lives—why shouldn't I?"

I swallow hard. "It's not the same. We'll be together. You shouldn't have to go off alone."

His gaze catches mine. The sudden sadness there steals my breath. "How much time did you have to spend on your own with no one to depend on? At least I know I have friends to come back to if I can escape."

Jostein makes a rough sound. "We can increase your chances quite a bit. We still have a few horses here. If you're riding, it'll be easier for you to evade capture. Tell them you don't want to get any more involved and ride off in a different direction from the town at first so they won't see you circle back toward us. That'll make it easier for you to approach them as if you weren't with us too."

Landric blinks at him. "You'd give me one of the horses…"

A tense smile that still holds some warmth curves Jostein's mouth. "I'll give you *my* horse. Come on, let's get you ready. You'll want to be well away from the mountain when you prepare to make your approach."

He brushes his hand across my arm in a fleeting farewell, his quick smile to me a promise that he'll take care of the man I still haven't decided how to feel about. They walk off into the darkness.

I take a few steadying breaths, not wanting to admit to myself how conflicted Landric's offer makes me. Why shouldn't he put himself in danger? Like he said, we all are.

Part of me aches at the thought of him falling into the Darium soldiers' hands, though.

I rouse myself from my uneasy reverie and move across the mountainside. After offering a few words of encouragement to comrades waiting to make the trek to Feldan, I reach Iko.

He's hunkered down on one of the flatter rocks, fiddling with a few bits and pieces I can't make out that he's balanced on his lap. I know he's spent the better part of the night working his gift, trying to use its inspiration to construct some kind of device that'll support our plan.

As I come over, he looks up. A smile that's only a thin shade of his usual grin flickers across his face. A strain I don't think is only from fatigue tightens his roguishly handsome features.

I'm not sure I've ever seen Iko really under stress before. I crouch next to him. "How's the inventing coming along?"

He sputters a hoarse laugh and adjusts the materials he's assembled: a canteen, some twigs he's whittled smooth and curved into circles, a few arrowheads, a chunk of lumpy vegetation. "Estera is making me really work for this one. I can picture how it could be once it's finished, but getting it there and actually moving..."

"You'll figure it out," I tell him with full confidence. "You always have."

"Hmm. Maybe a little extra inspiration from my spitfire will help."

He reaches out to me, and I tip forward to meet him.

The kiss he claims is more lingering than his usual playfully passionate embraces but equally sweet.

When he draws back, his smile has gone crooked. He hesitates. "You do *want* it to be like this, don't you? Being with both of us? If you'd rather stick with Jostein—Great God knows that'd be simpler for you—"

I cut him off with another kiss before he can go any farther. Who would have thought wryly confident Iko would be shaken by insecurities?

He twines his fingers in my hair, leaving them there when I pull back just far enough to speak, our foreheads still grazing.

"You and he are very different," I admit, "but I think that's why it's so hard for me to imagine my life going forward without both of you in it. Who else could make me laugh in the middle of the most terrifying mission I've ever taken on?"

A glimmer of Iko's typical slyness returns. "So I'm the jester in our trio, am I?"

I do laugh then, stroking my hand over his cheek. It's somehow reassuring that I'm not the only one who sometimes wonders if I could really be worthy of this much affection.

"The most handsome, clever, and charming jester a woman could ever ask for," I reply, and earn myself another kiss.

"Good," he says after. "I know I can be a little... forward. It's never intended to be pushiness."

"I'm not pushed around that easily." I sit back on my heels to contemplate his work. "Is there anything I can do to help before we have to move out?"

Iko considers his assembled items alongside me and pokes at the lump of vegetation. "I think this lichen is going to be the key. It's growing in patches around the mountain—

I'm not sure how much we'll come across after we leave. If you could gather as much as you can find in the next little while..."

"I can do that."

"Here, take a little piece so you know what to look for."

The lichen is bristly against my fingers, with a lacy pattern to its growth and a blueish gray color when I squint at it in the faint lantern light. Iko hands me a small cloth bag to collect my bounty in.

I set off across the rocky slope, heading higher up where the clusters of my comrades won't have disturbed the terrain as much.

It's difficult to spot the patches with no illumination except moonlight. We've left a few lanterns burning to reassure the Darium army that we're still barricaded up here, but I don't dare carry one and risk them wondering what my purposeful movement is about.

Instead, I bend close to the uneven rocks and press my hand to the darker splotches that stand out against the pale gray stone. Sometimes I encounter just gritty dirt, here and there a patch of moss. But on a few occasions I feel the same bristly texture as the lichen Iko gave me. I pry those patches free from their rocky home and drop them into the bag.

After the fourth, my heart starts to beat faster with the sense that the next peal of the hour should be coming soon. I pick my way down the mountainside toward the final stragglers of our camp.

The jangle of a bridle and a dry voice saying, "Hey there, Landric," bring me to a halt. Peering down the slope, I make out a glint of Landric's ruddy hair just beyond the reach of the nearest lantern, maybe fifty paces below me.

He's standing next to Jostein's stallion, who's fully tacked up. The squad leader must have moved on to other business after arranging the steed. But a couple of men from Feldan, guys around our age who I've seen Landric passing time with when Rupert and his noble associates weren't around, are ambling over to join him.

Mattias and Pascal. They were part of our childhood games too, back when we had little more to worry about than how to entertain ourselves.

"I heard you're riding off on us," Mattias says, his low voice traveling faintly to my ears.

I waver on my feet and decide it's better if I don't interrupt. Landric will be on his way soon enough. I sink down behind one of the jutting spires of stone where I can watch the conversation but they're unlikely to spot me in the darkness.

What will he say to them about his mission when the rest of us aren't around?

Landric speaks with impressive calm considering that he might be riding off to his doom. "I'm making sure our latest plan bears as much fruit as possible. If everything works out, I'll see you in Feldan before mid-morning."

Pascal snorts. "So you really are going to chat with the Darium army? What kind of madness is that?"

"Signy's madness," Mattias remarks before Landric can answer. "That crazy bint has gotten us pretty far, but gods above, that's got to be more thanks to the captains and their soldiers than her."

My hands clench at my sides, but Landric's voice simply flattens in its steadiness. "If we'd left it up to Major Arlo and the captains, we'd be handing ourselves over to whatever mercy we think the Darium empire might supply in the morning."

Pascal snorts. "That doesn't mean you have to stick *your* neck out farther than anyone else. How'd she convince you to take on this mad quest?"

Landric adjusts his hold on the horse's reins, swiveling

away from his friends. "It was my idea. She tried to talk me out of it. You should focus on your own part—I'd better get going."

Mattias steps back, but he elbows his companion. "You know, the crazy ones can really be something in the sack. I could see angling for a piece of that. But who would have thought Landric would get so desperate he'd go riding to meet an army just to land one lay with a—"

Even as I flinch, Landric whirls around. I don't see his fist flying until it slams into Mattias's face.

Mattias staggers backward, clutching his nose. Even in the dim moonlight, I see dark streaks of blood dribbling down his chin. "What the fuck was that?" he snarls.

Landric's voice comes out fierce. "That's for you to shut your babbling mouth. I don't know who you insulted more —her for not being worth more than a lay or me for being the type that'd treat a woman like a piece of meat—but if I hear any of it again, I'm not going to stop with one blow."

I think his friends are gaping at him with as much shock as I am. Pascal hisses a breath through his teeth. "You're turning on us over that—"

"Don't say it," Landric warns. "You don't even know her. You never tried. She lost so much, and you all..."

He shakes his head. "She's incredible, and I love her, and maybe at least I'd have seen it sooner if everyone hadn't made a hobby out of spewing garbage about her. But I know now, and I'm not going to listen to another word against her. Go get ready for your hike."

Mattias sputters something incoherent, but they both stomp off.

I might be worried about what they'll do next, but it's hard to believe they'd expect the Darium force to be friendlier than Landric has been. And I'm too busy staring at him as he tests the girth on the stallion's saddle one last time.

He has no idea I was listening. He told them off because he really believes all that. And he didn't care how it might change their opinion of him.

The jagged place inside me that's always stung when I talked to him, broken by the years of dismissals and snubs, melds together into something softer.

It isn't so hard to accept when I've seen it with my own eyes, is it? How much have I changed since the moment I decided I'd rather stab a Darium soldier than watch my mother's statue be destroyed?

This rebellion has changed Landric too. Brought out a courage and selflessness maybe even he didn't know he had in him before.

He grasps the pommel, and the realization hits me like a jolt of lightning that he's about to ride off into the midst of the enemy, possibly to his death, and I might not get another chance to speak to him.

I shove to my feet and pelt down the slope as fast as I dare, lifting my voice in a hushed but urgent call. "Landric, wait!"

He halts, surprise stuttering across his face as it whips toward me.

"I'm going," he says, presumably thinking I've had renewed misgivings. "I need to do this."

I skid to a stop just a couple of paces away, my heart thumping wildly. "I know. I just—"

I've already kissed two men in the past hour, but why *should* I stop there? If I'm going to be mad, I might as well go all in.

Closing the last short distance between us, I touch his cheek and bob up on my toes to press my mouth to his.

Landric's breath hitches, and then he's kissing me back with an urgency that shivers through my veins. He slings his free arm around my shoulders to tug me closer.

I drop my head against his shoulder, grappling with the urge to beg him to stay after all. "You'd better make it back to Feldan."

A soft chuckle tumbles out of him. He hugs me tight, as if he can't quite believe I'm in his arms. "I was always planning on it, but I'll be twice as determined if this is the welcome I'll get."

Both of us know there's no time left. He caresses the side of my face and steals one more kiss, his eyes shining with joy. Then he hefts himself into the saddle and sets off along the side of the mountain so he can circle the camp at a distance.

I watch him go with an uneasy weight expanding in my belly. Should I have accepted his proposal to go down there? Is it really worth the risk?

After all the battles I've fought in the past several days, I still can't say which the right ones are. Bloodshed and corpses were never what I wanted my legacy in this world to be.

As my throat tightens, a flutter of movement at the edge of my vision catches my attention. I turn and go still.

A butterfly is gliding along the slope. Its pale blue wings reflect the moonlight as if they're made of the stuff.

I've never seen a butterfly flying around in the night before. There are no flowers up here to tempt it.

Maybe it's some rare species that prefers the darkness, but a glow of hope lights inside me. Butterflies are one of the symbolic animals of Inganne.

It could be my godlen is offering me a sign.

Tapping my fingers down my front in the gesture of the divinities, I pad cautiously after the creature. It swoops here and darts there... and lands on the flat of a sword one of my comrades set down next to their pack.

I gaze down at the beautiful insect for a few seconds, taking in the way its wings shimmer against the sharpened metal blade, the interplay of delicacy and might.

If this is a message, then I think I understand it. There can be a sort of art to warfare, if you play it right. In the end, it's all a sort of game, after all, just one with the highest possible stakes.

Tomorrow I need to create a picture striking enough to carry my whole country through to freedom.

A town bell rings in the distance. The butterfly twitches and soars away.

I square my shoulders and march over to join the last of my colleagues, ready for the journey ahead and everywhere it might lead us.

CHAPTER TWENTY

Signy

Jostein surveys the outer walls of my cabin with an unreadable expression. "So, this was your home after you left your aunt and uncle's house."

I nod, my arms coming up to hug myself loosely. In the thin early morning light, the weathered logs and crooked door seem more depressing than I remember.

Iko steps closer to me and presses a kiss to my temple. "Hey, it looks a damn sight better than the rest of the buildings in town right now."

His teasing tone manages to bring a smile to my lips, if a bittersweet one. The Darium soldiers missed my cabin in their fiery rampage—not bothering to venture into the woods, I guess. All the structures on the familiar streets have crumpled into blackened cinders.

I glance instinctively toward the treetops in the direction of the hill that held our memorial. They didn't skip those stone walls, even though they couldn't burn them. The limestone slabs lie scattered and cracked across the hilltop.

We'll pay them back today. Whether it changes the course of Velduny's future or not, they'll know their brutality has its own consequences.

I run my fingers through my hair, still slightly damp from the quick dip I took in the river. Maybe we should have stayed by the water's edge, enjoying the peaceful burbling while we can.

But I'd wanted to see whether my old home was still standing.

"It wasn't so bad living here," I say. "No one usually came out this way, so I had the spot to myself away from the judgments. I learned a lot, having to find and hunt my own food, mend any tools I needed."

Jostein slips his hand around mine. "I suppose it's hard to say I wish you'd lived differently when I don't know who you'd be without what you've endured. But I hope we can make every day from here forward bright enough to erase some of those old hurts."

I squeeze his fingers, smiling at him and then Iko. "You already have. I can't regret anything that brought me to you."

Iko beams back at me. I think he's going to dip farther to claim a deeper kiss, but at the same moment, the crackle of the underbrush brings the three of us whirling around.

My pulse only has the chance to lurch once before I recognize the gleam of coppery hair on the approaching figure. Relief sweeps away every other emotion I was feeling.

Landric, looking no worse for wear than he did when he rode off several hours ago, comes to a stop at the edge of the glade. "Captain Amalia said you'd gone over to the river. When I didn't find you there, I thought this was the next most likely spot."

He pauses, his gaze traveling over the cabin and its surroundings: the scruffy patch of garden overgrown with weeds in my absence, the mossy outcropping of stone with the crevice that holds the tools I've scavenged that our neighbors discarded as trash. His mouth tightens.

Jostein keeps his hand in mine. "You delivered your message to the duke's son?" he asks.

Landric jerks his attention back to the squad leader. "Yes, and a good portion of the Darium force there as well, since I was yelling it from a distance. It's a good thing I had your horse—thank you. They definitely would have preferred to hold me for further questioning."

He tilts his head back toward the town, where most of our remaining resistance is gathered. "A couple of sentries reported in right after I arrived. It sounds as if my 'warning' had the intended effect. The Darium soldiers at the lake haven't started to march yet, and they sent a messenger toward the border. The rest of the army under High Commander Livius is approaching, but they won't reach us for another few hours yet."

I exhale in a rush. "Good. Then the people working their gifts will have more time to prepare the area."

Our magic-blessed allies have already thinned and weakened the stone beneath the earth across about a half-acre of land at the edge of the town, but the more distance we can cover, the more of the army we can topple in one blow.

Landric smiles. "I thought you'd want to know as soon as possible."

He pauses, and I find I don't know how to answer. The memory of our kiss last night and the things I overheard him saying clashes with the presence of the men I've already embraced as my lovers on either side of me.

Jostein and Iko said they'd welcome Landric, but how exactly am I supposed to handle this?

In my uncertainty, Landric's stance turns awkwardly stiff again. He dips his head as if to take his leave, and a protest leaps to my throat.

He's had to witness me in the arms of these two men more than once—and handled it more gracefully than most rivals for a woman's affections would. How can I say I care about him if I'm not willing to put the shoe on the other foot?

He loves me. He said it last night, even if not to me. I don't know if the ache of emotion inside me can match that statement, but I need to show him how much he matters to me.

Before he can move, I release Jostein's hand and hurry forward. Delight glints in Landric's eyes in the instant before I grasp the front of his tunic and lift my mouth to his.

He cups the side of my face and kisses me like I'm a long drink of water after a day of riding. Even after I ease back, I keep holding on to him. "I'm so glad you made it back to us safely."

The corner of his mouth quirks upward, but his crooked smile is gentle now. "I knew I'd better not let you down."

When I glance back at the other two men, my heart thumps with a hitch of nerves. Jostein's posture looks a bit tense, but his smile is undeniably fond. And Iko is outright smirking.

"That's our woman," he says in a tone resonating with admiration—and promise. He looks at the cabin and then back at me. "We have a little time. What do you all say we make Signy's last memory of this place a happy one?"

There's no mistaking the suggestiveness of that question. Heat sweeps through my body to pool between my thighs.

Landric trails his fingers up my back, but his caress is tentative, as if he's wary of his welcome. Jostein's bright eyes darken with a smolder of desire.

The squad leader takes in my expression and must be able to see the matching desire in me. My lips part, but before I need to speak, he holds out his hand and speaks with the same commanding tone he brought out in the tent the other night. "I'd say that's a brilliant idea. Come inside, rebel maiden. You're ours—and no one else's."

A giddy quiver of agreement passes through my veins. I step toward the cabin, gripping Landric's hand to tug him with me in case he has any lingering doubts about whether he's a full member of our strange but incredible relationship.

Jostein opens the door, careful of its wobbly hinges, and ushers me inside.

The drafts that slip past the doorframe and around the curtains over the glassless windows have kept the air within fresh. With weeks past since I inhabited the space, the only smells that linger in the air are those of pine and moss.

After the cool night, the summer sun hasn't had much time to spread its warmth yet. Iko kneels by the small fireplace and retrieves a flint to light the kindling I left there.

As the flames crackle across the bits of bark and twig, he adds a couple of logs to the fire. The wavering light fills the room along with a waft of warmth.

With the three men around me in the cabin, the interior feels so much smaller than when it was just me. Other than the fireplace, all it contains are the mattress I made out of stuffed canvas with a couple of tatty wool blankets over top, a rickety table with a single chair, and a set of shelves fixed to the walls that hold my few dishes and pieces of cookware. I spent most of my time outside when I could.

None of my lovers appear bothered by the modest surroundings. Compared to the hasty camps we've constructed over the past several days, I guess solid walls and actual furniture are almost a luxury.

And they're too focused on me to give the rest of the room's contents much mind.

Jostein turns my chin toward him and claims my mouth. As his kiss consumes me, Landric nuzzles the other side of my neck and nips the crook of my jaw. Iko rejoins us, sliding his hands under the hem of my tunic to splay against my bare stomach.

"I barely got to see you last time in the dark," he says in a husky voice. "You deserve every bit of admiration."

He lifts the bottom of my tunic, and Landric grasps the other side to help peel it off me. My childhood friend grins at me, so much adoration shining in his eyes that my heart skips a beat. "Out of everything in the world I haven't experienced yet, there's nowhere I'd rather be than right here, exploring all I can have with you."

Even more affection swells inside me. I tug him in for another kiss.

Jostein strokes his fingers across my back. Iko flicks his tongue across the peak of my breast through the thin fabric of my undershirt before raising the chemise to take my nipple right between his lips.

I gasp into Landric's mouth, and he lets out a strangled groan. His arm loops around my waist, pulling me close.

The hard bulge already risen behind his trousers presses against my hip. The feel of it sends more heat coursing to my core, but none of my men appear to have any intention of rushing the moment.

Jostein and Iko remove my chemise together, and then the squad leader massages one of my breasts while his friend returns his mouth to the other. The currents of pleasure have me swaying between them.

As Jostein recaptures my mouth, Landric hooks his fingers around the waist of my trousers and drags them ever so carefully down. The fire's warmth licks over my bared legs, nothing compared to the hungry flame growing inside me.

Landric kisses a path down my thigh alongside his progress, sinking to his knees. Not to be outdone, Iko teases his hand along the waist of my drawers.

Jostein gives my lower lip a gentle tug between his teeth. I can't restrain a whimper.

I don't just feel adored. It's as if they're worshipping me, like I'm so much more worthy than a girl who was shunned by her chosen godlen.

As if I'm a lesser god myself, and they mean to honor me in every possible way.

Iko strips off my drawers with a stroke of my ass that sends a spark of anticipation rippling through me. He glances around, but Jostein takes charge first.

"Turn the chair around." He gazes down at Landric, a smile unfurling across his face. "You're in the perfect position to take care of her already."

A flush washes over my skin at his apparent meaning. Iko nudges me down onto the chair, and Landric guides himself between my splaying knees without any hint of hesitation.

I'd feel self-conscious about having my most intimate area open to the firelight before all my men's gazes, but there's only reverence in their expressions.

Jostein pushes my ass forward on the seat so I have to tip backward. As he cups my breasts from behind, Landric kisses my inner thigh on one side and the other.

Then he lowers his head right between my legs.

With the first press of his hot mouth against my sex, a rush of pleasure floods me. I have to hold myself back from bucking forward hard enough to hurt his jaw. As it is, I rock and pant through the melding of his lips to my clit and the sensitive flesh beneath.

Neither of my past lovers, brief as our dalliances were, ever offered this blissful act, though they were more than happy to push for my similar attentions. I had no idea it could feel so incredible.

Landric's pleased hum reverberates through my core, sparking renewed delight. He laps his tongue right between my folds and then penetrates me with two fingers. Even more pleasure spirals out from that most intimate touch.

As he grazes his teeth across my clit and pumps his fingers inside me, my other two men are seeing that no other part of me goes neglected. Jostein continues fondling my breasts and branding my neck with kisses while Iko massages my thighs and ass, easing up now and then to catch my mouth.

"You've taken on so much," Jostein murmurs by my ear. "Now we're going to take care of you completely. Let it all go."

His heated words and the tweak of my nipples between his calloused fingers send me careening over the edge. I shudder against Landric's mouth, and he flicks his tongue faster, working his fingers even deeper to a giddying spot I didn't know existed inside me.

With a cry, I unravel. Bliss sweeps through every inch of my body until I feel as if I'm glowing with it.

While I come down from the high of my release, Landric dapples kisses along my thighs. Iko lets out a chuckle. "I suppose since the new fellow tended to our spitfire so well, he deserves a little reward. If you agree." He pinches my ass teasingly.

I wouldn't have thought I could feel more desire than I already have, but the sight of Landric's flushed, eager face sets off a throbbing of need. The need to be filled. The need to claim this man as thoroughly as he's claimed me.

Without waiting for Jostein to deliver more orders, I slide forward and push Landric down on the floor, his head coming to rest on the edge of my makeshift mattress. My hands dip to fumble with the fastening of his trousers. "Off, now."

A breathless laugh escapes him. He squirms out of his pants and drawers as fast as humanly possible.

Landric's cock juts up between us, thick and hard. When I rub my slick sex against it, his head tips back with a stuttered groan.

Iko and Jostein have followed us. Jostein kneels beside me, twining his fingers with my hair. "I love seeing a lady take what she wants."

His friend kisses my shoulder blade, crouching close behind me. "Possibly the lady would want even more?"

He trails his fingers down to the crease of my ass, reminding me of his previous suggestion. A heady quiver passes through my body. "I don't know—I've never tried—but I would like to."

"Don't worry. I took the opportunity to prepare when it was offered. All we needed is a little oil."

He leaves for just long enough to retrieve something from the pack he left by the side of the cabin. I can't help grinding myself against Landric's rigid cock and then rising up to take it inside me where I'm craving it most.

Every inch he eases inside me is pure bliss. As Landric fills me, he lets out another groan. Pushing himself farther upright, he captures my mouth and palms my breast.

"You feel amazing," he mumbles against my lips. "This is the only place I ever want to be."

Iko returns to us, already shedding his trousers. He positions himself over Landric's legs behind me and smears a smooth liquid over my other opening. It warms quickly with the deft strokes of his fingers.

Each caress sends more of that thrilling sensation through me, heightening the blissful stretch of Landric's cock. I can't hold back a moan.

Jostein remains next to us, his gaze searingly intent. Even as Iko starts to stretch my back opening with tantalizing fingers, I can't help feeling the moment isn't complete.

I catch the squad leader's gaze, willing my eyes not to

glaze over with pleasure. "I need you too. Let me—let me taste you."

If I had any worries that my fumbling request would land awkwardly, Jostein's ragged breath and the hurried jerk of his trousers dissolves it in an instant. His erection springs free, as impressively large as I remember, the head already gleaming with arousal in the fire's glow.

As I lower my head to lick my tongue across that bead of salty liquid, his grip tightens in my hair. "Gods. Signy, you're a fucking miracle."

The craziest thing is I feel like one as I wrap my mouth around Jostein's cock, as I take Iko's into me from behind and sway over Landric's, welcoming all of them in deeper. So much love and lust blazes through me in the most potent mix I can imagine that it's hard to see it as anything but divine.

How could we have found each other like this amid all the chaos around us if not through some godly intervention? I don't know who to thank for it, but I couldn't be more grateful.

After years of slinking along the fringes, keeping out of people's way, I'm suddenly seen, accepted, *wanted* more than I ever dreamed of.

Landric sinks back on the floor, working over my breasts as he thrusts up into me. Iko matches his rhythm with a grasp of my hips to help me keep pace.

My head bobs up and down over Jostein's cock as we reach a faster tempo. So much ecstasy is whirling inside me that I'm aware of nothing but the sensations radiating through my body and the groans of my men as they speed toward their climaxes alongside me.

The symphony of pleasure expands into a roar of bliss that consumes my entire being. A moan spills from my lips to reverberate across Jostein's shaft. The wave crashes over me, pulling me under and then tossing me high.

As the shudders ripple through my body, Landric's thrusts turn jerky. He clasps my leg as he spills himself inside me, his gaze fixed on me as if I'm the only woman in the world.

Iko bows over me, following the two of us into release with a hot rasp of breath over my back.

I clamp my lips tighter around Jostein with a swivel of my tongue, determined to bring him with us too. He bucks into my mouth with a rake of his fingertips over my scalp. "Signy—I'm going to—"

He's trying to warn me so I can pull back, but I simply suck him down harder. With a choked sound, he loses control. The thick spurt of his cum fills my mouth. I flick my tongue along his length again as I swallow it down.

We sag into a sweaty, sated mess. For just a moment, the worries of the day ahead feel far away. Landric kisses my shoulder tenderly, Iko tucks himself against my side, and Jostein nestles his face against my hair as if they mean to make themselves my very own suit of human armor.

We will all be in plenty of danger in a matter of hours. But I've been fighting all my life just to *have* a life—to live it in a shabby place like this, scraping by.

Now, finally, I'm making something meaningful out of all that effort. Both in the strange passion I've kindled with these three men and the battles that have brought our entire country within reach of freedom.

It's not the works of art I pictured making, but maybe it's something even better.

We doze in our satisfied state alongside the murmur of the breeze and the chirping of birdsong beyond the cabin walls. It's almost peaceful until a voice splits the air from somewhere off in the forest.

"Jostein! Iko! The Darium troops are nearly here."

CHAPTER TWENTY-ONE

Iko

I hold up the modified crossbow so all eight of the colleagues I've been able to equip can see it. "You fit the three arrows here, here, and here. When you pull the trigger, they'll all fire. So make sure it's only enemies in front of you, hmm?"

The other soldiers nod, their eyes alight with a mix of fervor and fear. The Darium army is marching on us from two sides now, both of them visible to our people who've been keeping watch from the hill at the north side of town. The contingent who ambushed us at the lake is coming from the south while the army we've tangled with twice before approaches from the east.

They aren't bothering trying to hide themselves with illusionary magic now. Possibly the mages they called on for help are too worn out after pushing their gifts to the limit yesterday. Or possibly they have us so outnumbered they don't see the need for stealth.

They want us pissing our pants at the thought of what will happen when all those skeleton-uniformed figures descend on us.

My colleagues with the triple crossbows spread out along the line we're holding at the edge of town. The burnt houses offer a tiny bit of shelter with the remains of walls and heaps of rubble.

I move to the larger cluster of allies I've equipped, this one a mix of soldiers and civilians who are good with various kinds of bows. We've had a lot of armor damaged or outright ruined in the past few battles, but I was able to see ways to work with some of the shields that've been cracked. They might not provide perfect protection, but by carving out a wider gap toward the middle, our archers can fire while remaining mostly protected.

"Aim quick, line up the arrow, and fire," I remind them. "Keep as much of yourself behind the shield as possible. You're part of our first line of defense, and you need to be visible, or they might not take the bait."

For Signy's plan to work, we need the Darium army to storm right up to meet us at the town. If they try to turn this into another siege like at the mountainside, holding back from the network of caves the gifted among us have worn away at under the earth, we'll have to take greater risks to provoke them.

As the archers position themselves with apprehensive but determined murmurs, Captain Amalia strides through the wreckage of the town to join me. She surveys the makeshift army we've held on to, all of them braced for the fight they know is coming.

The captains and Major Arlo have been laying out the bits and pieces of our strategy since early this morning. But now that the part Signy suggested has been carried out, we all know that by far the most vital piece comes down to me and *my* gift.

"They're no more than a half hour out," Captain Amalia tells me. "You're completely ready?"

My gaze flicks to the crate holding the five contraptions I was able to assemble from the materials we had. I've tested them out as far as I could without destroying them, but it's the final step that matters the most.

All of my knowledge and the nudging of my gift tells me they should work. Jostein stopped to check on my progress as I was fiddling with them and told me he believed I could pull it off.

Somehow even that partly divine assurance hasn't totally settled my nerves. What if he's confusing his hopes as my friend with his gift's ability to evaluate me?

Despite my worries, I grin at my captain. "I've gotten everything as prepared as I can before the actual explosions. If they don't work, we'll just have to hurl some rubble at the army and hope for the best."

Amalia is a good captain. She considers me and must pick up on the uneasiness I'm hiding, but she doesn't prod it. She simply claps me on the shoulder. "You've got one of the cleverest minds I've ever encountered, Iko. It's been a pleasure ordering you around, even with your mouthiness."

A laugh sputters out of me, and a little of the tension in my chest relaxes. "I'm glad to hear I haven't been giving you too many gray hairs. But I think Jostein deserves the largest portion of the credit here, at least among our squadron."

A smile plays with Captain Amalia's lips. "Your loyalty also gives you credit. Don't worry—Jostein's contributions haven't gone unnoticed. If we get out of this mess on top, they won't be unrewarded either."

As she walks on, my spirits lift at the thought that my friend might finally get the promotion he's been vying for.

Jostein might not have much patience for the politics of climbing the ladder, but he'd make a damn good captain—or even general—too.

A few shouts carry between the ruined buildings. I don't need to make out the words—I can see the cause right in front of me.

The Darium army has come into view over the top of the nearest low slope. The two forces are merging into one as they march toward Feldan. Even after we've battered many of them with blinding pollen and toxic wasp stings, they maintain their rigid discipline: strict rows in perfect step with each other, weapons raised in ominous rows.

Like a horde of the undead come to drag us to our graves. Even though I know the bones are nothing but white paint on black fabric, an icy shiver runs down my spine.

High Commander Livius rides in their midst, the several scarlet plumes on his helm standing out starkly amid the mass of black and white. He's chosen a ghostly white stallion, as if he's arriving on death itself.

My mouth goes dry. I pick up my crate and check over the contents once more.

Everything's there. It will work. I can spark the flame of our true victory.

I can make more than random gadgets of minor convenience. I can offer more than laughs and high spirits.

I've invented the winning blow to an entire war.

I've always known that between the two of us, Jostein is the real hero. But this once, I feel pretty heroic myself.

As long as I time this right.

As long as the blasted things do what I intend.

I owe it to Jostein, to my captain, to all my comrades— to Signy, most of all. We have to see this brilliant plan through.

The moment the Darium soldiers come within range, our

longbow archers let loose an initial wave of arrows. They thud into raised shields, but we didn't expect to take anyone down with those.

We just want them to know we're in an aggressive mood. Make them think it's better to deal with us once and for all.

Some of those soldiers will have been drawn from forts around the country. They won't want to leave those areas less protected for very long.

Come on, fuckers. Come right to us.

The Darium army halts. We remain crouched amid the wreckage, visible but not easy targets.

High Commander Livius's arrogant voice thunders across the field between us. "You have no hope of winning this fight, rats. This is your last chance to surrender. Those who continue their treachery should expect a very painful death."

No one budges. We all know death is the most we can expect by handing ourselves over to the assholes now.

We'll take our chances, thank you very much.

The high commander lets out a scoffing sound and motions to his troops. Their rows of archers tramp forward first, tall shields protecting the infantry behind them. They're not bothering to waste their arrows when we've got a decent amount of shelter.

Our archers send out several more shots, a mere heckling. They don't provoke an immediate retaliation, but I think the approaching soldiers pick up the pace just a little.

They're all pressing forward, the whole mass of them passing onto the target area. Not quite enough of them yet, though.

Major Arlo gives a wordless holler, and most of our forces draw back as if we're retreating into the ruins for additional cover. As if we intend to carry out this final fight amid the burnt buildings and not on the field.

I scramble behind a derelict wagon we left on the fringes to disguise my preparations and reach into my crate.

Each of the five contraptions is little bigger than a mouse. They'll dart like the vermin the high commander compared us to, skimming across the ground between our enemies' feet.

If we'd hurled similar devices at the army from above, those skilled archers could easily have shot them out of the sky. I need the impact as close to the ground as possible.

I lay them out in the shadow of the wagon, pointing at five different angles toward the march. Then I grip my flint.

The Darium soldiers bellow in a wave of threatening war cries. A few enemy arrows careen amid the retreating figures around me, knocking one of my comrades and another into the dirt.

Just another ten paces. Another five. Another one…

I strike the flint and let the sparks catch on the bits of moss protruding from the back of the contraptions. With a hiss, the shifting parts set the pairs of tiny wheels into motion.

My explosive speedy mice hurtle from beneath the wagon into the midst of the marching army.

I scramble backward behind a fragment of a stone wall. There's a startled bark and a crunch as one of my inventions must be spotted and stomped on.

But only one.

The moss burns hot and fast. I brace myself for disappointment—and the flames hit the mixture in the tiny, oil-drenched pouch at the middle.

The pouches burst in a series of small but fierce booms and spurts of the soil churned up by the impact. The surrounding soldiers yelp, several of them toppling.

And that's it.

I freeze, dread chilling my gut.

Then the very earth creaks.

The thinned, cracked rock beneath the surface shudders with an expanding groan, the precarious balance overthrown. A smile crosses my face.

Even as shouts of alarm ring out amid the army, the solid ground they were walking on collapses in a brutal crash.

CHAPTER TWENTY-TWO

Signy

At the first rumbles of explosive fire, I peek out from behind the crumpled shed I was using for cover. My breath snags in my throat.

Hundreds of Darium soldiers have barged onto the field just outside town, the nearest of them just steps from the buildings. But their rigid lines are falling into disarray.

One clump of dozens of bodies careens down with the collapsing of the earth. Then another and another around the spots where Iko set off his explosive devices.

The effect of the initial collapses shakes the ground all the way to where I'm crouched—and more of the earth opens up, sending the soldiers tumbling. The cave-ins ripple outward as if the grassy plain is a lake with one massive stone dropped in the middle of it.

Skeletal-uniformed figures collide in a jumble amid the jutting stone edges of the underground caves. Some slump, blood seeping through their helms from cracked skulls. Others groan, their limbs splayed at unnatural angles.

They thought they were bringing death to us, but instead it's come for them. Their uniforms couldn't look more fitting. It's as if a pit of corpses long dead and withered to bones lies before us.

I couldn't have created a more stunning picture with all the paint in the world.

And I *did* create this tableau. I imagined it and I brought it into being—for the men and women still fighting alongside me, for all of Velduny.

Even as awe sweeps through me, my body tenses, my fingers tightening around the grip of my short sword. The Darium force was too large for us to take out *all* of them this way.

For every body mangled in the cave-in, at least one other figure is scrambling back from the still crumpling edges of the earth, reaching to offer help to the nearest fallen, or rushing around the edges to deal out vengeance for our trick.

High Commander Livius's horse stumbles under him, the ground cracking beneath the animal's feet. As it goes down with a broken leg, he springs away before he can take any wounds of his own.

Seeing him and his ridiculous plumes still uninjured, I grit my teeth. But we have a more immediate problem.

The Darium infantry still standing hurtles around the edges of the pit. Arrows fly from our archers' bows, some of them launching forward in sets of three from the crossbows Iko doctored.

It's not enough to have conquered half the army with our scheme. We need to destroy every one of our enemies that we can.

We need them convinced that it's not worth continuing to fight us—that our rebellion is going to defeat them. That they'll lose so much more than they stand to gain.

Several Darium soldiers jerk and sag with arrows

protruding from their chests. Others charge onward into the ruin of the town.

I leap up and throw myself at the nearest attackers. The lessons Jostein and Iko offered me guide my sword arm. I manage to duck beneath the swing of a blade and plunge mine into a man's gut.

As I kick him aside, a woman in Darium armor rushes at me with a screech of anger. I lash out at her with my sword and bash her helm with a slab of burnt wood from amid the wreckage. When she sways with the impact, I slice my blade across her throat.

The spurt of blood makes me recoil. I clench my jaw and will my nausea down.

She'd have done the same or worse to me if I'd given her the chance.

All around me, my comrades are cutting down the attackers as well as we can while the archers continue to shoot some before they can reach us. The edge of the pit crumbles more, tossing unlucky soldiers into its depths.

A yell I recognize as Landric's voice brings my head jerking around. I spot him farther along the edge of town, slamming his elbow into the side of a soldier's helmet. The soldier jabs out with his spiked club, but to my relief, Landric drives his sword home faster.

It isn't only the enemy facing slaughter. Near me, one of Jostein and Iko's colleagues teeters over with a spear protruding from his throat. The Darium blades gouge into chests and limbs, sending blood spraying across the ruins of my town.

I jump in to ram my sword through an attacker's back just before he stabs a woman he's knocked over, but right next to us, another Darium soldier guts a teenaged boy who only joined our rebellion a few days ago.

Before I can raise my sword again, Jostein is there,

driving his longer blade into the man's side. As the attacker slumps over, the squad leader catches my gaze with a hint of worry but a nod of resolve.

We're seeing this through. We're going to keep fighting as long as any of us are still standing.

I swivel around, bracing myself for another onslaught. At the same moment, the high commander's voice bellows over the fray with its magical amplification.

"Pull back, soldiers! To me!"

He's calling for a retreat already? I don't know whether to rejoice or curse their cowardice.

His soldiers swarm around him at a safe distance beyond the pit. They appear to have given up on any of their colleagues who are too injured to pull themselves out of the cave-in.

With a few orders I can't make out, High Commander Livius assembles his remaining troops back into their strict lines. Though dwindled greatly from their initial horde, they still make for an imposing force, maybe three times greater in number than our ragtag band.

There's no way we'd face anything but a bloodbath if we tried to challenge them out there on open ground. We've only kept a bit of the upper hand by drawing them to us and using the ruins to our advantage.

Is the high commander going to turn this battle into another stand-off? Try to wait us out? We're much better situated here than we were on the mountain. We've got the river to turn to for water and fish, the forest for berries, nuts, and hunting, a little shelter from the elements amid the crumbled houses.

If they give us time, our gifted allies who prompted the cave-in might be able to weaken the ground farther out, right under them...

Even as I think that, the high commander lifts his voice

again, obviously intending it to carry. "We'll march on Piam and then Segward. Let's see how the rest of Velduny enjoys this rebellion."

Gasps and disgruntled hisses escape my comrades. A chill wraps around my lungs.

Those are the two towns closest to here—the towns where our neighbors who weren't up to fighting have taken refuge.

He means to slaughter every civilian he can, probably to torch their homes like he did ours.

The soldiers are already turning, heading to the west. High Commander Livius strides along behind them like a brutal shepherd guiding a flock of wolves. He shoots one cruel smirk over his shoulder in our direction before pulling the visor of his helm back down.

No. I can't let the victory that was within our grasp turn into a horrific tragedy.

I glance around for something, anything that might help. Through the blare of panic and desperate resolve, my gaze snags on one of the horses that's made it this far with us, tied to the burnt frame of a house.

There's no room for thought, only action. I bolt for the animal as if my life depends on it.

But my life isn't the one I'm concerned about. There are so many others that stand to be lost if we don't stop this tyrant of a high commander.

I yank the reins free and heave myself onto the horse's back. Someone calls my name, but the thrum of my pulse drowns out so much of the sound I can't identify the voice.

I dig my heels into the stallion's sides, and it leaps into a gallop.

We careen around the pit, the thunder of hoofbeats echoing my racing heart. I clutch the hilt of my sword, holding it at my side.

This may very well be suicide, but someone has to do it. Someone has to add the final details to the picture of our freedom.

I started us on this path, and I'll see us through to the end.

A few of the Darium soldiers glance back and then hesitate. The last few rows turn as if to meet my charge. High Commander Livius spins on his heel almost casually—

And I hurl myself right off the saddle into him.

The force of the collision sends him crashing to the ground with me on top of him. I'm already raking my sword through the air, the blade slashing through the leather covering his shoulder.

He grunts and lands a punch to my jaw that leaves my head reeling. When he shoves me, I slam my knee into his groin.

We tumble sideways, my elbow jarring against the ground. My sword slips from my fingers.

I smack my forearm against the side of his head hard enough to bang his helm off-kilter. In his temporary blindness, his hand closes around my throat.

And my groping fingers catch my sword again. Sputtering for breath, I whip it around and ram it straight through his neck.

The high commander sags over me with a gush of blood. Shouts bellow from all around me—a blade swipes through the air less than an inch from my ear.

I wrench out from under the crumpled body, yanking off the high commander's helm with one hand while I brandish my sword with the other. The Darium soldiers gape at their fallen leader for just an instant before they step toward me.

I hold the plumed helmet high as I ready myself, but more hoofbeats pound behind me. A stallion whirls by, a familiar muscled arm slinging around my chest and hefting me up.

"Here we are again," Jostein murmurs in a ragged but still wry voice as he swings me in front of him. "No respect at all for your own safety. Well, show them all what you've done, my dear rebel."

Breathless and blood-drenched, I lift the high commander's helm even higher. The sunlight glints off the black-and-white metal with its ruddy plumes.

Several other soldiers on horseback, including Captain Amalia, have ridden into the fray with Jostein. A few dozen archers and swordspeople are sprinting over at their heels. As they clash with the Darium soldiers, war cries splitting the air, my display seems to rouse the rest of our allies.

Over a hundred more figures burst from the ruins of the town. Whether they're waving swords or cooking knives or sharpened branches turned into spears, their eyes flash equally fierce. They tear across the field toward the Darium soldiers with the furor of an army ten times our size.

As Jostein circles us around, I see our enemies already faltering. They've lost hundreds of colleagues to us, they've lost their high commander, and now they're facing the full brunt of our long-bottled anger.

Blades clang and arrows hum through the air. First, it's just a few soldiers at the back of the Darium contingent backing away. Then, all at once, a chunk of them peel off and scramble for safety.

Those of us on horseback dive into the battle. Jostein stabs and slashes on one side of his horse while I lash out with my sword on the other. I kick one soldier in the face and carve open another's throat.

"Pull back!" one of our enemies hollers in a strained voice. "Regroup at Fort Sirus."

The remaining Darium soldiers stagger away from our

onslaught and simply run. Arrows and thrown daggers harry their backs. The rebels around me let out a jeering cheer of triumph.

Jostein lowers me from his horse at the same moment as Iko and Landric push toward us from different directions. My other lovers catch me between them in their arms.

"That was incredible," Landric mumbles. "But gods, you terrified me."

Iko guffaws. "That's our woman."

I hug them close, but a deeper urge draws me away from them. I stand a little back from the milling crowd and thrust the high commander's helmet into the air once more.

My ragged voice rings out across the plain. "We're just as strong as them. We don't need to be ruled. We can choose our own destiny!"

Another cheer goes up, and more of my comrades close in around me with grateful words. We're surrounded by the chaos of violence and destruction, but my heart couldn't feel lighter.

I've always wanted to bring beauty into the world, and I can't imagine a more stunning scene than this.

Chapter Twenty-Three

Several months later

Signy

My silky dress rustles around me as I shift on my feet. Everywhere I look, mosaics of swans and roses and swaths of pink draped across pale marble meet my eyes, making it impossible to forget exactly whose territory I've wandered into.

The Temple of Blissful Devotion is the largest temple in all of Velduny dedicated solely to Ardone, the godlen of love and beauty. We figured if we were going to request her blessing for a rather atypical sort of love, it'd be best to do it in her most prominent worldly home.

But now that I'm here, surrounded by all those symbols of divinity, I can't suppress the jitter of my nerves.

I drag in a deep breath of the perfumed air, scented by the very real roses that grow all around the airy building.

Jostein comes up behind me, tucking his arm around my back.

He must be able to pick up on my worries. He leans in to press a tender kiss to my forehead. "We don't *have* to do this. Not now, not even ever. Getting Ardone's approval won't change how much any of us love you."

I twine my fingers with his. "I know. But it makes a difference to the rest of the world."

For everyone who's accepted my joint relationship with three men, there are others who mutter scornful gossip and shoot disdainful glances our way. Never terribly overt, because I am still hailed as a hero of the rebellion, but I notice it and I know my lovers do too.

I never want them to have any opportunity denied to them because of their association with me. I want the whole country to see that the gods themselves support our shared affection.

But what if they don't? What if Ardone feels I've asked for too much, that I'm not worthy of monopolizing not just one but three incredible men?

Well, I've never been one to back down from a challenge, even those seemingly impossible.

As I square my shoulders with resolve, Iko and Landric amble over to join us. All three of my men have dressed up for the occasion like I have, them in formal jackets and trousers that set off their stunning looks to impressive effect. Taking them all in, I have to catch my breath.

"Getting cold feet?" Iko teases, giving one of the loose tendrils of my hair a playful tug.

I laugh. "Not at all."

Landric holds my gaze with all his usual intensity, his dark eyes never failing to send a tingle over my skin. "No matter what happens, we'll be by your side."

I reach to grip his hand as well and aim a determined smile at Iko. "And I'll be by yours. I love you all so much."

If that's not enough for the godlen dedicated to love, what could be?

With her blessing, we can properly marry. Our bond will be treated as just as valid as any other official partnering.

And I can confirm the love that's solidified between us over the past several months in the most unequivocal possible way.

One of the devouts in his pink robe of worship approaches us, tapping his fingers down his front in the gesture of the divinities as if to bring his chosen godlen to the conversation with him. "It's time. You can follow me."

Gathering myself, I walk into the main atrium of the temple surrounded by my men. Light in shades of pink, red, and purple beams down through the panes of stained glass on the domed roof overhead.

Several more devouts stand in a ring around the edges of the atrium. The one who brought us leads us before the cleric who presides over this temple, who's waiting by an altar at the one end.

The cleric bows her head to us with a soft smile that's also faintly sly. Ardone's worshippers are advocates for all sorts of romantic love, from the most innocent to the most carnal.

"Are you ready?" she asks.

When we all nod, she spreads her hands toward us. "Signy Mauddaut of Adelay, Jostein Silvansson of Nalbrecht, Iko Gerholdsson of Nalbrecht, and Landric Klausson of Adelay, you come before our passionate godlen today to seek her blessing for your union—one between the four of you instead of a partnering of two. What would you say to Ardone about your association?"

Jostein speaks first, with the commanding tone that provokes a giddy shiver down the center of me. "Signy owns my whole heart. My love is great enough that I welcome the love others can offer her as well."

Iko trails his fingers across the small of my back. "I've never cared for anyone else like I do for Signy—and I love seeing how much joy she experiences with Jostein and Landric as much as what she feels with me."

Landric shoots me a quick but fond smile. "I spent most of my life knowing I was missing something but too afraid to pursue it. Now that I've found my place with Signy, there's nowhere else I'd rather be. And what we have wouldn't feel complete without these two men who've become my greatest friends."

Now it's my turn. My throat closes up with a swell of emotion before I manage to summon the words, raw with truth. "I never knew how much love I was capable of until we found each other. What I feel for each of them seems incredible on its own; to feel it all at once three times over is a blessing in itself."

Did that come out all right? My men seem to think so, all of them beaming down at me. The cleric's expression gives no indication of approval or concern.

She tips her face back to the multi-colored light and raises her hands. "I have given my blessing to many couplings in Ardone's name—man to woman, man to man, woman to woman. To so bless four in their shared union, I reach out to the godlen herself. Ardone, if you would exalt this love, please give us a sign."

I have no idea what to expect. The gods normally work in subtle ways. I wait, my heart thudding, unsure how long we have before our relationship is declared unsanctioned after all.

Then a shadow passes through the sunlight streaming through the dome, like a puff of cloud. The pink-tinged beams swirl and intensify in a ring around the four of us for a few fleeting seconds before it expands back into its previous diffuse glow.

My lips part in awe. When I look at the cleric again, her eyes are open, sparkling with happiness. "Ardone has welcomed you into her embrace. You may go forward with all the same respect and consideration as any other union."

A laugh both startled and relieved tumbles from my mouth. Iko catches me in his arms and whirls me around. The moment he lowers my feet back to the ground, Jostein and Landric draw in around me in a joint embrace of our own.

The cleric lets out an amused hum. "I think you can celebrate a little more ardently than that."

Before I can get out so much as another giggle, Landric has accepted that challenge by planting his lips eagerly against mine. I've barely recovered from that dizzying kiss before Jostein swoops in. Not to be left out, Iko waits for his turn and dips me over with the melding of our mouths, his arm firm against my back.

"Come on," Jostein says, nudging his friend. "Let's go share the news."

I raise an eyebrow at him. "Share it with who?" The cleric and all the devouts serve as our witnesses if we need to prove Ardone's acceptance, but I didn't think we needed to worry about that immediately.

Iko simply grins. "You'll see."

We step out of the temple, and my jaw drops.

Tables have been set up amid the rose gardens that surround the temple lawn. They're laid with pitchers of ale and wine and platters of food—and surrounded by a few dozen guests I hadn't known had arrived, their expressions bright with anticipation.

Landric slips his arm around mine, and Jostein lifts my other hand into the air. "Ardone has blessed our love!"

At his announcement, a joyful cheer rises up from our spectators. Captain Amalia, standing near the head of one of the tables, waves us over. "Let's get on with the celebration, then!"

As we descend the temple stairs to join the merriment apparently in our honor, I spot several of my old neighbors who I fought alongside until the final driving of Darium influence from our country a couple of months ago, a bunch of Jostein and Iko's colleagues, and even the new duchess who replaced Duke Berengar.

The last of those glides over to offer her congratulations. She bobs her head to me as if I'm the one with the greater name here. "I'm so pleased to see the four of you receive all the acknowledgment you deserve. If there's ever anything you need that I might be able to supply, please don't hesitate to reach out."

She meanders off, leaving me blinking at her back. Iko chuckles and bumps his elbow against mine. "Don't look so surprised. She wouldn't have her job if it wasn't for you."

I guess that's true in a way. Shortly after our confrontation with the Darium force at Feldan when I cut down High Commander Livius, the royal family of Velduny began rallying all the country's troops to join our rebellion. King Manfred and Queen Rinka hadn't been able to do much for Velduny while under the emperor's watchful eyes, but they jumped at the chance to win the country back once and for all.

And when they heard about how Duke Berengar and his family had sided with the empire, they were rather displeased. As soon as the war was won, they stripped them of their titles and elevated a different local noble family in their place.

I find myself gripping a glass of wine in one hand and a pastry in the other, overwhelmed by the flood of well-wishes.

It's been obvious that people appreciate my part in the rebellion, but other than an intimidating meeting with the king and queen themselves to receive a token of honor and a promise that they'd call on me again soon, the past two months haven't been particularly eventful.

Everyone might have been busy pulling their lives back together and deciding what they'll make of themselves with our newfound freedom, but that doesn't mean they've forgotten how we got here.

A smile crosses my lips. I offer my thanks to everyone who approaches us, nibbling my pastry in between.

"You're going to be even more celebrated soon, if that's possible," Landric tells me. "The bards are just starting to present their first compositions recounting the Veldunian Quest for Freedom."

Jostein shakes his head. "And they have taken some liberties too—only in your favor, from what I've heard so far. One version has you charging down a hilltop straight at the emperor himself."

I snort. "Emperor Vitus was never even here."

Iko shrugs. "They enjoy making their stories as epic as possible. I don't see any problem with that." He leans closer and steals another kiss. "I'm honored to be one of the few who knows the whole, true story of our reckless, unshakeable Signy."

"Hear, hear," Landric says in agreement, grinning.

I beam back at all of them, basking in the warmth of their affection, and raise my glass. "And here's to all the other stories we still have ahead of us."

Thank you so much for reading *Heart of Defiance*! I hope you enjoyed this glimpse into the Abandoned Realms.

If you'd like to spend more time in that world, I have two series set in this world so far! In Rites of Possession, follow a thief with forbidden magic who becomes known as her country's Signy when she tackles a dark conspiracy that threatens her entire kingdom (while falling in love with four hot but damaged men). Start that series with *Thief of Silver and Souls*:

In The Royals Spares, venture into the heart of the Darium Empire, where an underestimated princess enters a series of deadly trials to protect her conquered country and marry the emperor's heir... but finds herself falling for the hostage princes who are his foster brothers (and totally forbidden). Start that series with *A Game of Veils*:

A GAME OF VEILS EXCERPT

1

The carriage has just crested the last low hill before the imperial capital when the spring breeze sours with the stink of rotting flesh.

Our driver exhales sharply and clucks at the horses to pick up the pace. My stomach knots.

The sight beyond the window can only be disturbing, but I need to face everything that lies ahead of me.

As I reach for the curtain, Cici makes a soft noise of protest where she's sitting on the opposite bench. When I tug at the fabric regardless, she simply closes her eyes.

At first, the narrow view shows only scattered farmhouses amid golden fields beneath the clear blue sky.

Then a post comes into view next to the road.

A corpse dangles, limp feet hovering over the ground, a head with blood-caked hair sagging. What skin I can see is purpled and torn by the beaks and teeth of scavengers.

The largest gouge was clearly made by a sword. Someone

carved open this man's front from throat to groin to let his innards spill out in a gruesome display.

It's a reminder from Emperor Tarquin of what happens to those he believes threaten his empire.

Whatever the man's crimes, he wasn't alone in them. More posts stand in a row with his, each holding a body ripped apart in the same way.

The one beside him wears the remains of a dress. His wife? After her, another in trousers, and finally—

A form barely half the height of the others, tiny hands with mangled fingers, a crimson-splattered ribbon unraveling from pale hair.

I shut my own eyes then, clenching my hand against the urge to clamp it to my mouth. Willing down the surge of nausea that roils in my gut.

Cici won't judge me for my horror, but I'll be surrounded by those who will soon enough.

When I'm sure my arm won't shake, I tap three fingers to my forehead, heart, and belly in acknowledgment of the nine godlen who watch over us. Those lesser gods are the only divine power we can appeal to.

I finish the gesture of the divinities with a clasp of my hand over my sternum, where my skin beneath the bodice of my dress is branded with the sigil of the one godlen I specifically dedicated myself to.

Elox, I think in a silent prayer, *may their souls be at rest and let me bring healing to this place.*

Whatever that family did, I can't accept that a child deserved such brutal punishment.

The godlen of medicine and peace doesn't respond, but then, I've never met anyone the gods have spoken to directly. That isn't how they work.

A tendril of calm unfurls inside me as if in a gentle caress. My shoulders straighten in response.

I will not be shaken from my purpose.

When I open my eyes, the butchery beyond the window has passed behind us. The putrid stench is fading away.

Cici shoots me a tight smile, her sallow face looking slightly greenish. "His son could be different."

I allow myself what might be my last fully honest comment before the imperial palace swallows me and my maid up. "Let's hope so."

Should a woman be happier than this on her way to her wedding? In some ways, I am pleased.

I've spent twenty-one years standing on the sidelines, watching my country suffocate under the empire's thumb. Knowing it's my older sister who'll rule after our parents—as much as anyone in our family rules with the limited authority our conquerors allow us to keep—and that my primary value is in the loyalties my marriage can strengthen. All I could do was wait and find out what man I'd end up tied to.

For the first time, I'm contributing something to our kingdom, to my people. And it's more than I ever could have dreamed possible.

Somehow my parents arranged a betrothal to the most powerful bachelor in the continent: the heir to the entire empire.

Given Emperor Tarquin's reputation, agreeing to their proposition must have been an entirely strategic move on his part. He's tying my distant country more deeply into the empire, enforcing my parents' and my sister's loyalty for decades to come.

Gods only know what other factors motivated him to accept the offer. This is a man who thinks stringing up mutilated children is a reasonable law enforcement tactic.

But his son, Marclinus, is a separate person. He isn't the one enforcing the laws... yet.

I'll keep an open mind. Find the best in the situation I've been presented with.

If the imperial heir will listen to me, I could give every citizen of Accasy a better future.

I fold my hands together on my lap, my thumb sliding over the rippled gold of the ring on my left forefinger. The impression rises up of Mother squeezing my hands when we stood in the castle courtyard just before I left.

You are wanted, she said, *and that is a kind of power. Don't let them strip away who you are. Trust in your gift.*

When she hugged me, the tremor that ran through her slim frame contradicted the confidence in her words.

The halt of the carriage tells me we've reached one of the gates into Dariu's massive capital city. When the driver produces his papers with their official seals and announces that he's escorting Princess Aurelia of Accasy, the guards wave us onward.

One aims a leering glance through the window as the wheels rattle by. I pretend I'm too distracted by the looming buildings to notice.

I've heard that over a hundred thousand people reside within Vivencia's walls. It's hard to wrap my head around that number when Accasy's largest city contains less than a third of that number.

Plenty of the citizens are going about their business on the stone-paved streets. They stroll past tenement buildings, duck in and out of shops, and lean on their window ledges to bask in the mid-day sun.

Everyone I see looks contented enough. I suppose as long as their actions don't clash with the emperor's plans, he treats the people of his own country benevolently.

Why order them into back-breaking labor or let his soldiers run wild among them when he can exploit those he's conquered instead?

As we weave between the tall buildings, the breeze dwindles. The spring warmth turns to mugginess within the confines of the carriage.

I swipe at the long brown waves of my hair in an attempt to cool the perspiration beading on my neck. Cici tuts at me and leans over to tidy a few particularly errant strands.

Back home, I'd have had my hair pulled back in clips or braids to keep them out of my way. Why does a country with a significantly hotter climate make a fashion of unmarried women keeping their hair loose?

When I left Accasy, the air still held the crisp freshness that arrives with the spring leaves. I could have walked into the dense woods beyond the castle if I was seeking a deeper cool relief.

The homesickness wells up inside me so abruptly I nearly choke on it.

It's a long trek north. I can't imagine my future husband will be all that enthusiastic about regular visits.

A lump rises in my throat, but I swallow it down.

It doesn't matter. I'm entering this marriage to free my people from the worst of the tyranny, even if I'm not there to see them thrive.

I still have my memories to hold on to, whatever else happens.

Cici peers outside with wide eyes. "The city's so *big*. I wonder how far it is to the palace?"

The maps I studied swim up through my memories. "The imperial compound is at the south end, by the river. We'll have to pass through a lot of Vivencia to get there."

"I guess that gives us some time to take a look at the place." She offers me another smile, this one softer around the edges.

I return it with a pang of gratitude. We're both venturing

into unknown territory. The uncertainty is easier to bear with a companion on the journey.

Cici came on as my maid just four years ago. She's always kept a certain respectful distance, but she's gamely aided when I'm working on a concoction and never grumbled about how many hours I spend outside like my childhood maid used to.

Maybe once we're caught up in the imperial court together, we can become something more like friends.

The buildings on either side of the broad road grow taller and more sprawling. We pass an expansive park of grassy fields, flower beds, and fountains amid only a few stately trees. Men and women in flowing jackets and dresses meander along the paths or ride on horseback.

After passing a few more grand estates, we stop at another gate.

It takes our driver longer to make his case for entry into the imperial palace grounds. Finally, our horses draw us past elaborate hedges and a towering sculpture of Creaden, the godlen who presides over leadership and justice. He's been carved with the imperial crest clasped in his hands: a majestic hawk soaring over a grand oak, with the motto *CONQUER ALL* framing them.

That statue is followed by several life-size busts of imposing men and women I assume are past emperors and empresses. Then the carriage turns with an arc in the drive, and the palace comes into view.

I find myself staring at the three-story building of silvery marble that could encompass my family's castle ten times over.

My jaw goes slack before I can control my shock. In the first instant, I can only stare at the massive columns carved with leafy designs and the lofty windows reflecting the glare of the sun.

As the carriage rasps to a halt, several men in the purple-and-gray imperial livery stride down the stairs outside the yawning palace entrance. A few move to the back of the carriage to retrieve my two trunks. Another places a step beside the carriage while his colleague opens the door.

Girding myself, I paste a smile on my face, gather my silk skirts, and ease out into the tiled courtyard.

The stoutest of the staff, a jowly man who looks at least ten years older than his apparent underlings, is waiting for me. He dips his head in a motion of deference that's not quite a bow. "Princess Aurelia. It's a pleasure to welcome you to Dariu and His Imperial Majesty's home. I hope your journey went smoothly."

He speaks in Darium, of course, knowing I'll understand. Every royal throughout the empire learns the language of our conquerors alongside our native tongue.

At his question, the image of the corpses hanging by the road flits through my mind. I hold my smile in place. "Quite, but I'm certainly glad to be at the end of it."

"We'll first be—" He cuts himself off to frown at Cici, who's positioned herself beside me with her own bag by her feet. "Was there something you needed from your mistress before you return?"

Cici blinks. "Return? I'm Princess Aurelia's maid, sir." She dips into a brief curtsy.

"And I'm sure you've tended to her well during her travels," the emperor's man says evenly. "But His Imperial Majesty prefers to select all the staff who work within these walls. The princess will be assigned a very capable maid of our own."

My stomach sinks. Cici darts a nervous look toward me.

If we argue rather than accepting the supposed generosity, will the emperor suspect some ulterior motive?

What are the chances he'll bend his usual policy for a woman he barely knows, soon-to-be-wife of his son or not... rather than string Cici up at the side of the road as punishment for our defiance?

I speak cautiously. "We weren't informed. My parents assumed—"

The stout man cuts in with a brusque tone. "She and your driver can inform them of the arrangements when they return. You should find our hospitality warrants no complaints."

The note of warning in his words sends a sliver of ice down my spine. I'd *better* not complain.

I don't want to start off my time here on the wrong foot. Or see an innocent woman harmed simply because it wrenches at me to lose the comfort of her presence.

I touch Cici's arm in reassurance. "It's fine. Tell my parents that Emperor Tarquin is taking care of everything for me."

Her expression stays worried. I dip my head in a slight nod, holding her gaze firmly. "Safe travels."

I'll be all right. I was born for this.

She gives my hand a quick squeeze, her eyes shimmering with sudden tears, and then one of the footmen is ushering her back into the carriage. I watch it pull away with a tearing sensation in my chest.

Now I'm utterly alone.

The man who greeted me clears his throat. "His Imperial Majesty is eager to welcome you personally and introduce you to his court."

Including his son, my future husband. We had better get that over with.

My smile might be a little stiffer than it was before, but I follow my escort through the immense doorway obligingly.

I will not tremble. I will not falter.

I'm a joyful bride thrilled to have made such an incredible match.

And if a whiff of hysterical laughter bubbles inside me at that thought, I certainly won't let it out.

Inside, the imperial palace is just as overwhelming. The central hallway sprawls as wide as my bedroom at home. The ceilings loom far above my head, painted with vines and flowers framing open sky as if to give the impression they aren't ceilings at all.

I suppose the spaciousness makes sense given the difference in climate. Accasians prefer narrow halls and cozy rooms that are easy to keep warm during the frigid winters. These airy open spaces must be much cooler during the southern summer.

More marble gleams everywhere I look, alongside panes of etched gold, delicate mosaics, and oil paintings of majestic landscapes. Flute music carries faintly from up ahead, mingling with distant laughter. Potted plants with crimson and fuchsia blooms give off a heady floral scent.

Our footsteps tap across the tiled floor until we reach a set of double doors framed with gold. My escort marches a few paces ahead of me and declares my arrival to the room at large: "Princess Aurelia of Accasy!"

Clearly my impending arrival was noted well in advance. The vast audience hall I step into holds dozens of people, all turning to watch my approach.

Most of my audience is gathered on either side of the violet rug that runs the length of the room. The men and women wear similar clothes to those I saw in the nearby park: gauzy dresses and silky shirts.

I wore my lightest gown in recognition of the warmer weather, but it seems to drag against my limbs as I make my way past their curious stares.

On the dais I'm heading toward, two gilded wooden thrones gleam, their backs pointed in elegant spires as if to mimic the crowns on their occupants' heads.

In the larger throne in the middle of the dais sits a tall man with a sharp-edged face and a pale scalp nearly as shiny as his seat. I've heard Emperor Tarquin took to shaving off all his hair as soon as it started to thin.

His eyebrows, just below the rim of his ornate golden crown, are such a light blond they blend into his skin, giving the eerie impression that he has none at all. A suit of black, gray, and indigo covers his sinewy frame.

As I force my legs to keep moving toward him, his steady gaze pierces straight through me.

I drag my attention away from the emperor's ominous presence to the younger man in the throne at his right.

This has to be Marclinus. A matching if simpler crown adorns his hair, which is nearly the same shade of gold as the metal. His angular features echo his father's, though much more appealing with some lingering softness of youth.

Unlike his father, he sprawls in his throne as if he's lounging at a tavern rather than conducting an official audience. His golden-blond curls drift carelessly across the tops of his ears and down to the nape of his neck.

When our eyes meet, he licks his lips.

That's how he greets his future wife?

The emperor is flanked by a few pensive-looking middle-aged figures I'd guess are advisors of some sort, one of them in a cleric's robes. Beyond the imperial heir's throne stand four men too young to have likely risen to such prominence. Three of them can't be much older than me, and the other looks to be in his teens.

Who are they? As far as I know Emperor Tarquin only has one son, and they don't look anything like him besides.

The tallest fills out his silk shirt with broad shoulders

bulky with muscle. The cream-colored fabric sets off his tawny skin. His dark brown hair is pulled into a short ponytail at the nape of his neck.

His eyes, so light blue they're noticeable even from a distance, sear into me along with his scowl.

The leaner but still well-built guy next to him has a rich brown complexion in starker contrast with the imperial men. His thick black hair appears rumpled even cropped close to his handsome face. His dark eyes follow me, his hands balling at his sides.

Their somewhat shorter companion looks as if he's been denied a few meals. There's a hint of gauntness to both his pale face and his frame. But his features are still striking, his reddish-brown hair and deep green eyes giving his expression a kick of intensity. He's folded his slender arms tightly across his chest.

Even the teenager is glowering at me from beneath the fall of his white-blond hair. His gangly limbs make me think of an overgrown puppy, but his fierce expression is all guard dog.

What about me has provoked all this hostility?

I jerk my attention back to the emperor and stop a couple of paces from the dais. There, I drop into my lowest curtsy.

I need to stay focused on the man with the real power here.

"It's an honor to be in your presence again, Your Imperial Majesty." I've only seen the emperor once before—a brief introduction when he toured his territories when I was six—but he'd expect me to remember that.

The emperor's smile is as sharp as his face. "Welcome to my court, Princess Aurelia. Let me formally introduce you to my son, His Imperial Highness Marclinus."

He sweeps his hand toward the lounging, golden-haired

man, who sits up only a little straighter and gives me a jaunty wave. His eyes, the same gray as his father's, slide down my figure as if he's stripping off my gown with them.

The corner of his mouth quirks upward in what's closer to a smirk. "I think I'll enjoy making *your* acquaintance."

Great God help me, this is the man I'm supposed to live out my days with?

Emperor Tarquin doesn't appear fazed by his heir's attitude. He motions to the figures at his left. "The key members of my cabinet and all of my court look forward to celebrating your arrival." He tips his head toward the crowd around the room and pauses before glancing beyond his son as if he'd almost forgotten who else was present.

"Ah, and my foster sons: Prince Bastien, Prince Raul, Prince Lorenzo, and Prince Neven."

Foster sons? All princes?

Before I can even start to puzzle out that statement and his dismissive tone, the emperor goes on. "Given that your family suggested this match, I assume you've come willingly, Princess Aurelia."

I bob my head again. "Of course, Your Imperial Majesty."

"Refresh my memory and confirm what I was told. How old are you?"

"Twenty-one."

"And you're where in line to the throne of Accasy?"

"I'm my parents' second child, Your Imperial Majesty." Does he really need to hear me rehash all this?

Emperor Tarquin lets out a low chuckle. "The full title can become a mouthful. I give you permission to simply call me 'Emperor' for the duration of this conversation."

"Thank you, Emperor."

He lifts his chin toward me. "Which godlen have you dedicated to, and did you make a dedication sacrifice?"

I'm not sure how much detail he's heard from the imperial representative who conducted the betrothal negotiations, but I have no reason to obscure my answer. Nearly everyone in the realms dedicates themselves to one of our gods at twelve years old in the typical ceremony. It would be a shock if I hadn't.

At least half of the people I've met, nobles and commoners alike, took the greater opportunity presented by the dedication ceremony. It's the one chance we have to be blessed with a gift of magical talent. But of course we must offer something of ourselves in return.

"I dedicated to Elox," I say. "I sacrificed my spleen for a gift for making healing potions and other cures."

The emperor's eyebrows rise. I can't tell if he's genuinely startled or putting on an act to try to loosen my tongue. "A medic princess. That might be a first."

I give him the simplest honest explanation I can. "I wanted to be able to help people. I can't heal anyone directly, though, only concoct things that can."

"And have you faced any adverse consequences from the loss of your organ?"

I think of the tiny scar on my stomach. "Nothing significant. Illnesses tend to hit me harder and take longer to recover from, so I'm careful to look after my own health as well."

"Very wise."

The back of my neck prickles with the sense that he's subtly mocking me, but Emperor Tarquin leans back in his throne as if he's satisfied. "You appear to be exactly who we were promised."

I summon my brightest smile to cover my next lie. "I'm glad to have pleased you and look forward to my marriage with great joy."

The emperor rubs his thumb along the point of his chin.

Something in his expression sets the hairs on the back of my neck on end before he even opens his mouth.

"*If* you marry. Let's not be hasty."

What does Emperor Tarquin mean, and why are his foster sons so hostile toward Aurelia? Find out in *A Game of Veils*:
https://mybook.to/GameofVeils

About the Author

Eva Chase lives in Canada with her family. She loves stories both swoony and supernatural, and strong women and the men who appreciate them.

Along with *Heart of Defiance*, she is the author of the Royal Spares series, the Rites of Possession series, the Shadowblood Souls series, the Heart of a Monster series, the Gang of Ghouls series, the Bound to the Fae series, the Flirting with Monsters series, the Cursed Studies trilogy, the Royals of Villain Academy series, the Moriarty's Men series, the Looking Glass Curse trilogy, the Their Dark Valkyrie series, the Witch's Consorts series, the Dragon Shifter's Mates series, the Demons of Fame series, and the Legends Reborn trilogy.

Connect with Eva online:
www.evachase.com
eva@evachase.com